HAWAIIAN Holiday

Ten strangers, six days in paradise, one unforgettable Christmas.

MICHELE PAIGE HOLMES

Copyright © 2019 Michele Paige Holmes
Print edition
All rights reserved
No part of this book may be reproduced in any form whatsoever without prior written permission of the publisher, except in the case of brief passages embodied in critical reviews and articles. This novel is a work of fiction. The characters, names, incidents, places, and dialog are products of the author's imagination and are not to be construed as real.
Interior Design by Cora Johnson
Edited by Cassidy Wadsworth Sorenson and Lisa Shepherd
Cover design by Rachael Anderson
Cover Image Credit: Deposit Photos #57637083

Published by Mirror Press, LLC

ISBN-13: 978-1-947152-69-4

Other Books by Michele Paige Holmes

Counting Stars
All the Stars in Heaven
My Lucky Stars
Captive Heart

A Timeless Romance Anthology: European Collection
Timeless Regency Collection: A Midwinter Ball
Timeless Regency Collection: Wedding Wagers

Hearthfire Historical Romance Series:
Saving Grace
Loving Helen
Marrying Christopher
Twelve Days in December

Hearthfire Scottish Historical Romance Series:
Yesterday's Promise
A Promise for Tomorrow
The Promise of Home

Forever After Series:
First Light

Power of the Matchmaker series:
Between Heaven and Earth

Table of Contents

Chapter One: Shattered 1
Chapter Two: The Truth 7
Chapter Three: Hard Knock Life 11
Chapter Four: New Friend 25
Chapter Five: Pull of the Moon 31
Chapter Six: Thankful 35
Chapter Seven: Charlie 39
Chapter Eight: Observations 45
Chapter Nine: Possibilities 51
Chapter Ten: Not What You Think 57
Chapter Eleven: Watching 71
Chapter Twelve: Arrested Development 79
Chapter Thirteen: Tough Shells and Thick Skins 85
Chapter Fourteen: The Most 107
Chapter Fifteen: The Places You'll Go 109
Chapter Sixteen: Once in a Lifetime 123
Chapter Seventeen: Retail Therapy 131
Chapter Eighteen: O, Christmas Tree 137
Chapter Nineteen: Small Comfort 149
Chapter Twenty: Half a Man 155
Chapter Twenty-one: All is Calm 161
Chapter Twenty-two: Alternate Endings 165
Chapter Twenty-three: Leap of Faith 171
Chapter Twenty-four: It's Not Over Yet 175
Chapter Twenty-five: Santa is Polynesian 181
Chapter Twenty-six: Hail Mary 185
Chapter Twenty-seven: Good will toward men 191
Chapter Twenty-eight: The Joy of Giving 203
Chapter Twenty-nine: He's Got Legs 215
Chapter Thirty: Misunderstanding 219
Chapter Thirty-one: Soaring 223

Chapter Thirty-two: Almost Perfect..............................237
Chapter Thirty-three: The Love Boat...........................241
Chapter Thirty-four: Winter Wonderland...................245
Chapter Thirty-five: Even Better...................................251
Chapter Thirty-six: It's a Wonderful Life....................257

1

Shattered

HANDS SHOVED DEEP in his coat pockets, Gage Stevens crossed the park, his boots compacting the fresh snow with every step. The last vestiges of sun cast shallow rays over the path, as one by one the old-fashioned overhead lamps lit for the coming night.

He was late, for this party and especially for the news he was about to spring on his fiancée. He couldn't decide if he was glad Hailey and her family were still here, having their annual, epic Thanksgiving weekend snowball fight, or if it would have been better if everyone had been back at the house already. Certainly, he could get a moment alone with Hailey more easily here, at the sprawling Onadaga Park in Syracuse, but he worried about after, when she'd need her mom's arms or her sisters surrounding her, buoying her up by calling him all the lousy names he deserved.

"Gage is here, everyone!" Hailey's nephew Kyle popped up from behind a three-foot snowbank. "Hey, come be on our team."

From the corner of his eye, Gage saw the snowball flying his direction. Instead of following his instinct to duck, he turned toward it, catching the full impact of the slushy ball on his chin. Small penance for arriving so late. Completely inadequate punishment for what he was about to do. They could hit his face with a hundred snowballs and it wouldn't begin to alleviate his guilt.

"Nice one, boys. Just the thing to persuade Gage to be on your team." A few yards away, Hailey rose from her own shelter, built oddly around a park bench. "He's on *my* team, and you'll only make his revenge—and mine—worse by hitting him while he's in the neutral zone. If you mess up his face before our wedding—" She raised a menacing fist toward the boys, then waved the mittened hand in front of her, beckoning Gage to hurry.

He couldn't seem to make himself move faster, or fast at all. Each step filled him with more dread. In the year and a half they'd dated, never once had he not been eager to see her. They'd spent every minute they had together, had spoken or texted daily when they couldn't see one another. How he'd looked forward to those days of separation being over, to December 27th, when they would officially belong to one another. Their plans couldn't have been more perfect. They were going to run a business together, live together as husband and wife, and have a wonderful life. He'd never wanted anything more than he wanted to be with Hailey.

Even now, Gage felt drawn to her, couldn't have stayed away if he'd wanted to. But somehow, a few minutes from now, he would have to do just that.

A second snowball hit him, this one harder and in the back.

"Pelt him, boys! Make Gage pay for making Hailey wait."

Reed. Hailey's brother. If he had any inkling what Gage was intending—

—I'd be a dead man right now.

When Gage was still a couple of feet away Hailey reached out and grabbed the front of his coat. "You're so late. I've about frozen holding these guys off. My sisters took the little kids home, and I've been by myself the last fifteen minutes." She pulled him close and pressed cold lips to his. Instinctively Gage felt his arms going around her, then forced them to stop. He couldn't hold her anymore. *Get this over with. Get out of here.*

"Hailey."

She looked up at him through eyelashes dusted with snow. Her nose and cheeks were pink with cold, her breath making little puffs in the air in front of her. Concern darkened her eyes. "What is it? What's wrong?"

Gage knew exactly how her brow would be creased beneath her knit hat. "I—"

A flurry of snowballs came hurtling at them. She dropped to her knees, pulling Gage down with her, behind the bench. "Is it your mom? Is everything okay?"

His mom had spent Thanksgiving with them, here with Hailey's family, and he'd driven her home this morning. All had gone well until they'd pulled into her driveway this afternoon and he'd walked her to the door, then deposited her suitcase just inside. He'd given her a quick hug and let go a casual remark about how he and Hailey would spend next Thanksgiving here, and his mom might even have more than a new daughter-in-law to be excited about by then.

That hadn't elicited the reaction he'd expected.

Mom had pulled back from his hug, her hand trembling on the knob. "Oh, Gage," she'd begun, eyes filling with tears as her other hand came up to cover her mouth. "You don't know? He didn't tell you?" Her next words tumbled out in a torrent of apology and regret. A few simple sentences—one in particular he would never forget—and then it was over. The future he'd envisioned had crumbled around him, as tangible as if a pane of glass had shattered over his head. Blindsided, he'd stumbled to his car, backed up, then sped recklessly down the street like a teenager.

But there was no outrunning this. Over the course of his four-hour drive he'd examined it from every angle and concluded the only thing to be done. *The right thing.*

"No," he now said, as Hailey tugged at his arm and looked up at him expectantly. "It isn't my mom. She's fine."

He was glad it wasn't that, yet felt conversely sad that it wasn't. Not that he wished his mom ill. He just wished—He swallowed hard, pressed his lips together. How was he supposed to tell the woman he loved—

"Quit kissing, and start playing," Reed shouted.

Hailey jumped up and yelled back, her voice just as loud. "Give us a minute. No more snowballs until I say!" She planted hands on her hips and glared at her brother and two nephews, as if that might somehow make her five feet six inches appear more menacing.

"Ten-minute break," her dad called.

He's still here. Good. Hailey was going to need someone, especially if her sisters and mom had already gone home.

"Hot chocolate, everyone," her dad called. Members of Hailey's large family stumbled out of before-unseen shelters and out from behind trees, over to her dad and his hot cocoa station on the walk.

Gage stood and touched Hailey's arm. "Can we go somewhere more private?"

She turned a quick circle. "Sure. How about the gazebo? It doesn't look like anyone's there right now." Hailey inclined her head toward the pergola near the lake.

They left the marginal protection of her low-walled fort and trudged across the snow, deeper here than on the previously-shoveled path.

Behind them the battle continued, in spite of Hailey's

threat and her father's call for time out. Gage envied them their happiness. He envied them a lot of things, mostly just each other—all that crazy family of hers scattered throughout the park.

Gage didn't take her hand but followed her, at a safe enough distance that she couldn't reach back and take his. He didn't want to tell her like this, not here, not anywhere. His courage and resolve were slipping.

They stopped at the gazebo and faced each other. He looked down at her, rosy cheeked and trying to smile, though she bounced up and down on her toes—a sign of anxiety more than the cold.

Jamming his hands in his pockets so he couldn't touch her, Gage cleared his throat and began his carefully practiced speech. In the car he hadn't managed it without tears, but here, where it mattered, his performance went off without a hitch. He said what he had to, quickly and without emotion, then turned and walked away without looking back.

2

The Truth

HAILEY WALSH TWISTED the diamond ring on her finger as she stared out the plane window. *Blue—as far as the eye can see.* It was a fitting color, considering her mood the past month. Rather than thrilling at the beauty of the clear sky above and the sparkling ocean below, she felt weighed down by the sight. Nothing, not even Christmas in Hawaii, could lift her spirits.

Gage had crushed them. Permanently.

"That's a pretty ring you've got there."

Pulling her attention from the window, Hailey noted her seat companion for the first time. There was an empty middle seat between them—a perk, Hailey had supposed, of booking last minute and being seated in the last row of the plane. Apparently, though, it wouldn't provide the buffer of privacy she'd hoped for.

"Thank you." Hailey forced a smile, noting that the brunette about her age also wore a beautiful wedding ring. She probably had lots of reasons to be happy.

"Meeting your fiancé in Hawaii for Christmas?" the woman asked.

Yes. The lie was right there, along with the others Hailey had been telling herself since the day after Thanksgiving. *Gage is coming back. Something* must *have happened with his mom or health or work. He didn't mean what he said.*

Lying to this stranger would certainly be simpler than explaining the truth, and it wouldn't hurt anyone.

Except myself.

Hailey took a deep breath. It was time she faced reality. It was what this trip was about. Everyone thought she was using it to escape reality; but she needed the change of environment to help her deal with it. *Starting now.*

"Actually no. I'm not meeting him. In fact—" her chest constricted—"I'm not even engaged anymore." She managed the words without tears, though her throat felt like it had lodged a baseball. With a second, tight-lipped smile, Hailey turned back to the window, twisted the ring from her finger, and dropped it into her purse—where she vowed it would stay until she could fling it into the ocean.

"So, this is paradise?" The newest arrival stopped beside Gage, a duffle slung over his shoulder. He lowered his sunglasses as he took in the pool scene.

"This is it," Gage agreed with false cheeriness. *Paradise or purgatory.* Nothing like being in one of the most romantic places during a holiday all about home and family, and feeling utterly certain he'd never have someone to love or a family of his own. He leaned forward, arms braced on the low wall that surrounded the pool. What had his mom been thinking, gifting him this trip? That a week in Hawaii was going to make him forget Hailey and the happy life that almost was?

"Better selection than I expected," his companion said. "Couple of blondes, a brunette or two, and even a ginger."

Gage cringed at the flippant summary of the women in

view. *No wonder so many females hate us.* The thought no sooner entered his mind than he realized how hypocritical it was. Hadn't he, just a few weeks ago, given Hailey good reason to hate him and every other male she ever encountered?

He cleared his throat. "Did you, uh, read the fine print for this trip? It was pretty explicit about the rules for interaction with the opposite sex. There isn't really supposed to be any interaction, except at the organized outings and service expeditions." *Even then, no flirting, no overtures. No pairing off outside of scheduled activities.* Those rules were the only reason he'd agreed to come—that and the hope that pouring his energy into serving at an orphanage would take his mind off his troubles for a few days at least. But if this guy hadn't understood the program beforehand . . . "This isn't the place to meet someone," Gage said.

"Sure it is." His companion grinned, revealing a row of perfectly straight, ultra-white teeth. "What else do they expect will happen with five men and five women spending a week together in paradise? One for each of us, right?" He laughed at his own joke.

Gage shrugged, second guessing his decision to be here for at least the dozenth time. *It'll be good for you,* his mother had said. Right now that looked doubtful. Palm trees and sandy beaches aside, he was alone and would remain that way.

"Brock Coleman, from Ontario." The newcomer stuck out his hand.

"Gage Stevens." They shook. "Upstate New York. What part of Ontario? If you're near Toronto we're practically neighbors."

"Ontario, California, actually. I forget I have to clarify that when I leave the state. Guess everyone's not fortunate enough to live on the west coast."

"Guess not." Was this guy for real?

"Technically, I only work in Ontario now," Brock said. "About a year ago I bought a condo at Newport Beach. Heck of a commute, so I kept the place in Ontario as well. But most days I make the drive anyway. It's worth it to catch some good waves, you know?"

"Yeah." Gage knew he wanted to get away from this guy as soon as possible. He turned back to the pool, debating whether he wanted to nap on a lounge chair near the water and risk more unwanted company—possibly female, if the women felt the same way about the rules as Brock did—or if he should return to his room and stay there until dinner.

"Well, nice to meet you." Brock hoisted his duffle higher on his shoulder. "I think I'll go introduce myself to the redhead. Can't see much of her face from here, but those legs . . ." He whistled softly.

Against his better judgment, Gage allowed his gaze to follow Brock's. The woman's face was indeed hidden, by the latest edition of—the *Magnolia Journal.*

No. Gage blinked, then looked closer. Pale legs were crossed at the ankles, bare save for the glint of a silver anklet. Heart sinking, his eyes moved higher, searching for—the pink flamingo wrap partially covering her thighs. He felt his mouth open and gasped.

"I spotted her first, pal." Brock nudged Gage's shoulder as he moved off toward the steps leading to the pool.

One hand still braced on the pool fence to keep him steady, Gage used his other to whip out his phone. He hit his mom's number and waited for the call to connect. She'd barely said a surprised greeting when he started on her.

"I want the truth. Did you know?" He could hardly say it. "Did you know Hailey would be here too?"

3

Hard Knock Life

HAILEY TOOK HER smoothie out to the lanai and found a seat on one of the loungers where she could soak in the gorgeous sunset. After a minute or two staring out at the golden tones spreading over the lush greenery, she laid her head back, closed her eyes, and inhaled the sweet, heady scent that was north-shore Oahu. She'd been here once before, about ten years ago, after graduating from high school, and she remembered the scent of plumerias and the way the air had felt different the minute she'd stepped off the plane.

The fragrance took her back, to a time when life was simpler and possibility stretched out in every direction. She'd had goals and dreams and was going to reach them all. There was nothing she couldn't and wouldn't do.

She sank further into her lounger. A decade later, she could say she'd accomplished many of her plans. She'd graduated from college and was a successful interior designer. After working for a company in Syracuse the past four years, she'd struck out on her own, moving north to Chaumont, to live near the water and to start her own business, a Joanna Gaines-type store and design center in an old house on Main Street. It had helped her finances immensely that she was also able to live on the same property, in the upper story of the house. Buying the house with Gage had helped too. Never mind that she had yet to figure out how to keep it without him and seemed light years away from putting Chaumont on the map the way the Gaines had put Waco there.

All in good time. Or so she'd believed. Everything had been falling into place just as she'd dreamed. *Until Gage derailed it.* Without his architectural half of their team, she needed a new plan—a reboot—fast.

Hailey sighed, then sucked in a long drink of her coconut, strawberry, pineapple smoothie. A berry stuck in the straw. *A perfect metaphor for me—stuck.* She felt paralyzed, unable to move forward with her life, yet unable to return to how things used to be, before meeting Gage.

"Welcome, everyone. Welcome!" Lucy McIntosh, the forty-something program director, stood at the open patio doors, the smile on her face as bright as her yellow-and-red floral wrap dress. She looked around at the five women scattered about the lanai. None of them had spoken much yet. Rooms were private here, and, excepting the unwanted attention from one of the program's male participants, Hailey hadn't talked with anyone other than Lucy.

"Tonight we'll be doing introductions, along with a short presentation about tomorrow's service activity. If you'll all gather at the table, dinner will be served, and you can eat while I talk."

With reluctance Hailey left her comfortable seat and, disabled drink still in hand, made her way to the long table. At least tonight, it was women only. The men were eating somewhere else, and she was grateful. She hadn't come on this trip to meet someone. She'd come to find herself again. The contract she'd signed before coming had practically guaranteed she *wouldn't* meet anyone of significance while here. There wouldn't be time, and it wasn't encouraged. The purpose of the program, as well as the rules, had been outlined specifically. There was to be no pairing off, and therefore no pressure. Instead, Hawaiian Holidays, Inc., a nonprofit service organization, promised a joyous, meaningful, and unforgettable Christmas.

Hailey felt dubious about all three of those promises, but she hoped this week would be more bearable than being at home with her parents and siblings, their spouses and kids, and the general chaos that was her family. She exchanged polite smiles with the women on either side of her, then glanced across the table and was shocked to see her seatmate from the plane.

"Hello," the woman said, only kindness in her gaze.

Hailey smiled, grateful she'd told the truth to this stranger and grateful the woman didn't appear to think less of her for it. "Hello, again."

The patio doors slid open once more, and this time it was Micah, Lucy's husband, who appeared, with large, decorative platters of fruit held aloft in each hand. His biceps strained beneath the short sleeves of his worn surfing T-shirt, and his longish hair appeared windblown, as if he'd just returned from the beach. A few days' growth sprouted along his jawline, partially hiding an otherwise tan face. *The quintessential laid-back, north-shore resident.*

"Good evening, ladies. Tonight's chefs hope you enjoy your meal." He walked toward the table, followed by additional men, each bearing a platter or bowl.

"May I introduce our other guests this week." He set a tray of fruit at each end of the long table, then announced the names of those behind him as they delivered their dishes. "Caleb. Ray. Darren."

The three men nodded and smiled before moving quickly out the opposite doors. Back in the kitchen, Hailey heard terse voices, followed by Lucy's insistent one.

"Brock," Micah continued, as the man Hailey had had the misfortune to meet earlier reached the table. He set his platter down with a ridiculous bow, wave of his arm, and a wink in her direction. She scowled in return and hoped Micah or Lucy had noticed Brock's behavior. She'd never have come on this trip if she'd have thought there was any possibility of being hit on.

"*And* Gage," Micah said, with an encouraging look toward the doors leading to the kitchen.

The name alone caused Hailey's heart to jump. Just her luck, a guy named—

"Hi, everyone."

The jump turned to a skip, then a frantic beating. Against her will Hailey found herself turning in the direction of his voice. And, as if he'd expected just that, Gage—*her* Gage—stood there, his attention fixed on something behind her, as if she was invisible or didn't exist. Hailey's eyes smarted. Her palms pushed against the table, and she started to rise at the same second his gaze lowered and collided with hers in an almost audible connection.

How dare you be here.

What are you doing here?

Trying to pick up the pieces of my life.

I'm sorry.

For breaking my heart? Or for coming here to mess me up even more?

"That's everyone," Micah said, then cleared his throat.

As if just remembering where he was and that others were present, Gage pulled his gaze from Hailey and hurried out the doors to the yard.

Micah clapped his hands together. "All right, then. You'll be seeing each other off and on again through the week. Enjoy your evening, ladies."

Hands still clenched around the table, Hailey stared down at her plate, knowing that was the last thing she would do now. If she'd thought this challenging before, her success here seemed impossible now. How was she supposed to move on, with Gage in residence?

She dropped into her seat again and reached for her napkin, trying to pretend that nothing had happened, that she wasn't on the verge of tears. Head down, she counted silently to thirty—that birthday milestone approaching all too quickly, the one by which you were supposed to be successful in your career, married with two kids, and owner of a mortgage.

On autopilot, she dished pork and rice and some kind of noodles onto her plate, then passed the platters. She speared a piece of melon from the fruit tray and tried to think of doing the same to Gage. *Get angry, Hailey.* Any emotion would be better than the sadness she was drowning in right now.

Though the food was delicious, she picked at it, barely listening to the others' small talk. Everyone introduced themselves, but she forgot names or mixed them up almost as soon as they were spoken. There was a Lisbeth, Meghan and a Kristin. *Or was it Kirsten?* The woman she'd met on the plane and who was seated across from her tonight was Allyson. Privately Hailey decided Allyson was the most striking of all of them, with her long, dark hair and thick lashes framing beautiful hazel eyes. Hailey wondered why Brock hadn't bothered *her* at the pool.

Probably because she *has a ring on her finger.*

Lucy showed a slideshow next, about the orphanage they'd be visiting tomorrow. For a few, brief minutes, Hailey forgot her own woes as she learned about the plight of several of the children—all disabled and all from the islands of Polynesia.

"Your job this week—one of them, anyway—" Lucy paused to smile at everyone—"is to build a playground these kids can safely enjoy. We have to accommodate for the hearing impaired, blind, wheelchair bound, and mentally disabled. It's a tall order." She breathed in deeply. "Possibly made taller by the fact that some of the less-handicapped students will be helping us. We're all going to need a lot of patience to get this playground built and to not only allow, but encourage, those students to help with the building."

Lucy resumed the slideshow, and Hailey listened and watched the brief histories of each of the students who would be helping them. There were five in all, and they would be assigned to teams of two Hawaiian Holiday participants. One student was blind; another had cerebral palsy. Two had down syndrome; one was missing both legs. As each of the children's pictures were shown, Hailey found herself feeling sadder and sadder. What difficult lives these children had. What horrible circumstances many had come from.

Why is the world such an unfair and rotten place?

By the time the slideshow was finished and Micah had served hot fudge brownie volcanoes over ice cream, Hailey knew she was perhaps an hour away from a total breakdown—another one. They'd been happening about once a week since Gage had called off their wedding. Hailey hoped the walls of the women's bungalow weren't thin. Her ugly cry mode wasn't usually very quiet, and the last thing she wanted was company while she fell apart.

"Now that you've met the children we'll be working with this week, it's time we get to know each other a little better." Lucy closed her laptop and picked up a stack of papers from the end of the table.

Hailey closed her eyes briefly. *Please, no.* She couldn't bear it if the guys came back in. Even if they didn't, she wasn't up for any get-to-know-you games or meaningless chit chat. She just needed to be alone. Now.

She was about to raise her hand and plead an early bedtime due to a headache, when Lucy began speaking.

"Just as we got to know the children we'll be working with, it's important we know each other. Understanding what someone is going through or dealing with is the first step to feeling empathy for him or her. Research has taught us that people who are empathetic are more generous with and concerned for their fellow men. Why does that matter, some of you might ask? From a purely selfish point of view, it matters because those who exhibit empathy also tend to have happier relationships and experience a healthier personal well-being—exactly what we are about here at Hawaiian Holidays. While we want you to have a fabulous week here in paradise, we also want to send you home with the tools for a happiness that's sustainable. Something that I promise you *is* possible, regardless of your situation." Lucy paused, her smile faltering slightly.

"Odd as it may seem, we're going to begin with some sad stories to help get each of you to that happy place. I have short bios on all our participants this week—five of which I'll be sharing. Tonight is all about girl power. You'll have other opportunities to get to know the guys throughout the week."

This was starting to feel like a sleepover with a female Dr. Phil. From reading the website, Hailey knew Lucy was both a psychologist and licensed therapist, but somehow Hailey hadn't expected that to come into play so much and so soon.

I could have seen a therapist at home for a lot less. What she wanted out of this trip was some stellar experience, something breathtaking and beautiful that would remind her the world was a good place after all and would give her a reason to pick herself up, dust off her troubles, and carry on. Learning about kids with sad lives—and now hearing about women with the same—wasn't doing it for her. It might even make her crash sooner.

Outside it had started to rain, the pitter patter of drops sounding on the roof. Hailey felt her own storm and subsequent downpour coming, just minutes away perhaps.

She pushed her barely-touched brownie volcano away and started to rise.

"I won't be using anyone's names." Lucy glanced up, and her eyes met Hailey's. "So no one needs to worry about that. We're not after sympathy here, though that's not a bad emotion either. As I read these, what I want each of you to do is to imagine how this individual must feel. How would you feel in her shoes? It's important that everyone hears this. If you'll all please stay just a few more minutes."

For the second time that night Hailey sank back into her chair, attempting to make it appear as if she'd just been shifting to a more comfortable position. *More comfortable would be with my face buried in a pillow behind a closed, locked door.*

"I encourage you *not* to try to match each other tonight with the circumstances I describe," Lucy said. "You all applied to come here, and you all were chosen because we felt you had a good reason—a need for this program at this time in your life. As you listen, I hope you're able to recognize some of the common threads in each of your stories. I also hope you'll feel a little better about your own."

Doubtful. Hailey didn't see how hearing a recap of her sorry situation was going to make anything better. But she found she was curious, particularly about Allyson. What had brought *her* here?

"One of you lost your mother to pancreatic cancer five months ago." Lucy looked around the room at each of them, in such a way that Hailey had no idea who she might be talking about.

"A lot of people lose their parents or other loved ones to

cancer. It happens every day. Fortunately, the majority of those people have a good support system—another parent, a spouse, siblings, extended family. Someone who can grieve with them and see them through such a difficult time. The woman here who lost her mother has none of those. She's never met her father—doesn't even know who he is—and she doesn't have any other family. She described her relationship with her mother as follows: 'Mom and I were the real Gilmore girls. Sisters as much as mother and daughter as I grew older, best friends, our sole family to each other. I'm so lost without her.'"

Lucy paused, shifting the top paper to the bottom of the stack. "She has come to Hawaii for Christmas, simply hoping we can help her survive the holiday. I hope we all will help her do much more than that."

Wow. Hailey thought of her own mom, and the way she'd all but begged Hailey to spend Christmas at home, surrounded by her crazy family. She had nieces and nephews, sisters, a brother, a sister-in-law, and brothers-in-law in abundance. Cousins and aunts and uncles too. She felt like the family oddball, being the only unmarried one and having chosen a foo-foo career, as her brother liked to tease.

She'd heard their concerns before—both those spoken directly to her and those spoken to others in the family, when she wasn't supposed to hear. Her parents worried that she was all alone in Chaumont, unmarried, and without any kind of sustaining career. *No man. No money.* She'd had both until last month. And she still had enough savings for another six months to make a go of her shop.

And I have a mom to cry to if it doesn't work out. Hailey swallowed an uncomfortable lump as she recalled all the times she'd sat on her mom's bed in the weeks since Gage had unexpectedly ended their engagement. *What would I have done without her?* There was something about a mother's arms around you that was irreplaceable. No one could give comfort quite like that.

Hailey took a quick, surreptitious glance at the other women. In spite of Lucy's warning, not to try to figure out who was who, she wanted to know who had lost her mom. She wanted to know so she could step up and be a friend, at the least.

"Our next guest hasn't lost her parents, but it almost feels like she has." Once again, Lucy looked around the room, her eyes never lingering on any one person. It somehow helped to maintain the sense of anonymity, and Hailey found herself grateful.

"After thirty-three years of marriage, this woman's parents have recently divorced. This event is tragic enough, but to compound matters, there is so much bitterness and animosity between her mother and her father that this guest couldn't really spend Christmas with either. Not only would there be a decided lack of Christmas spirit if she did, but the parent she didn't spend the holiday with would be offended, angry, and hurt. What's a woman to do?" Lucy threw up her hands, then smiled. "Spend Christmas in Hawaii of course! We heartily welcome this guest and hope she finds much-needed peace while here, as well as a strategy for surviving in her new circumstances when she returns home."

Me too. Hailey felt both sympathy for the woman whose family was falling apart and a similar quest for peace in her own life. *Is this Allyson?* If so, why wasn't she with her husband? Or maybe she was wearing her mother's wedding ring. Maybe her mom had taken it off, and Allyson had claimed it, or was even keeping it safe, hoping her parents reconciled.

Possibilities filtered through Hailey's mind as Lucy shifted papers once again.

"One of you fought leukemia through much of high school." Lucy didn't look up this time but paused anyway. When she resumed speaking it was with a softer voice, one Hailey sensed she was struggling to control.

"At twenty-four this woman recently learned she has a brain tumor, and right after Christmas she'll begin treatment—much of which is often as bad or even worse than the disease itself." Lucy lifted her face, tears glistening in her eyes.

"You'll have to excuse me," she said. "I lost a little brother to leukemia, so this hits close to home." She swallowed, then tried again, her voice still catching. "By her own admission, this guest is almost more scared of the treatment she's facing than the very real possibility that she won't be able to beat her illness this time. So she's decided to fulfill one of the items on her bucket list—a trip to Hawaii—now, while she feels well enough to enjoy herself. She's told her family that she was invited here to spend the holiday with a friend. She doesn't want to ruin *their* Christmas by sharing her bad news, so she'll tell them after the holidays are over." Lucy swiped a hand across her cheek. "I hope she feels she has four of the best girlfriends in the world by the end of this week."

A brain tumor. A death sentence, or close to it. Hailey sat frozen in her chair, feeling almost physically ill herself. The women here had real problems—enormous ones. Hers had seemed that way, too, until a few minutes ago. But now—

"Our next guest has suffered the recent double whammy of having her heart broken and losing her business partner."

No! Hailey wanted to shout at Lucy to stop, not to bother with her stats. What was losing a business and a fiancé compared to losing your life? Or your mom? Your family as you'd known it? She felt her face heating. Why was she even here? Why had they chosen her, among these others with such serious problems?

But if Lucy caught her panicked look, she didn't let on.

"Just after Thanksgiving, and a scant five weeks before their wedding, this woman's fiancé broke their engagement. He gave no reason, but told her in an abrupt, one-sided conversation. Not only were they to be married in a matter of weeks, but they had recently begun a joint business together, purchasing a home both to live in and for this business, the future of which is more than unstable without both his partnership and financial contribution. Her life savings is already invested and dwindling fast. Even worse, her heart feels so broken she's not sure she'll ever recover.

"Her dreams of the future—from her wedding day to running her own, successful design shop, to a family of her own—have been swept away, leaving her reeling and uncertain about anything, especially herself."

Lucy took a deep breath and looked at them all. "She's in Hawaii hoping to find something to give her hope for a future, a reminder that all is not lost, that the world is a beautiful place, full of possibility—even when it seems all has been taken from us."

Hailey sat stiffly in her chair, staring straight ahead, hardly breathing. *Allyson will know it's me.* Would she tell any of the others? Would they all think her problems petty, comparatively?

Lucy began the last bio. Hailey half-listened as she picked up her spoon and reconsidered dessert. Right about now eating a volcano of chocolate seemed like a pretty good idea.

"After eight years of what she believed to be a happy marriage, this woman came home two months ago to find her husband and her best friend together—and they weren't having coffee. Like our last guest, she is suffering a broken heart, and she's dealing with betrayal too. She's lost her two best friends and feels more alone in the world than she ever has before. She didn't want to be by herself for Christmas, but she also didn't feel like she could face the holiday with her family, answering questions about her impending divorce and dealing with their advice and sympathy. Nor does she want to hear them telling her what a schmuck her husband is. She's seen firsthand proof of that, but she still loves him and would give him another chance if he wanted it. Eight years of love is a lot to throw away."

He *threw it away!* Hailey's mood swung wildly once again, this time channeling the anger she couldn't seem to summon for her own situation. Why should the cheater be forgiven? Whoever this woman was, someone needed to help her learn to let go and move on.

Kind of like I need to.

This is different. Gage didn't cheat on me—did he?

She'd wondered off and on the past weeks if that was what had prompted him to call off their engagement. *Had* he met someone else?

If so, why would he be here, and not off happily enjoying his choice?

Hailey couldn't believe that of Gage, but another possibility—that something was up with his health—seemed much more likely, after all she'd heard tonight.

Gage wasn't here for a pleasure holiday. None of them were. They were all in survival mode of sorts. Which meant he was trying to survive something big too.

4

New Friend

LUCY ENDED THE evening by thanking everyone for staying and encouraging them to think of others before themselves this week.

"Believe it or not, that's a crucial step to starting to feel better—for all of you."

Hailey could only think of Gage. *Why is he here?* She stabbed what was left of her volcano with her fork. *Why, why, wh—*

"I appreciated your honesty on the plane." Allyson dropped into the seat beside Hailey. "You have no idea how much it helped me to hear you say what you did."

Hailey looked up from the melted chocolate mess on her plate to see that the others had left the lanai and only she and Allyson remained.

"I wanted to thank you for your example," Allyson said. "It was courageous."

"Thanks, but I'm sorry, I don't follow." Hailey wondered how admitting that she wasn't any longer engaged qualified as an example of anything other than a failed relationship.

Allyson's smile didn't reach her troubled eyes. "I've been meaning to do this, only I couldn't bring myself to. Eight years *is* a long time." She pursed her lips in a grim expression and began twisting the diamond ring from the third finger of her left hand.

Oh no. Her husband and—her best friend. "I'm so sorry," Hailey began. "I can't imagine—eight years. Gage and I were only together about eighteen months, and I've wanted to die these past few weeks."

"I don't think the length of time matters." Allyson's ring came free, and she held it in the palm of her hand. "When you give your whole heart to someone, and they leave, they take it with them. And functioning without a heart is pretty impossible." Her fingers curled around the ring. "What are you going to do with yours?"

"I've considered flinging it in the ocean," Hailey admitted. "I thought that might be good therapy toward the end of the week—you know, symbolically leaving my past behind. How about you?" She nodded to the ring in Allyson's hand, noting a white stripe on the finger where it had been. *I should get her something else to put there.*

Allyson shrugged. "I don't know. I'm not even sure I can keep it off." Her voice cracked on the last word. "Because that means—it's really—over." Tears began to flow from the corners of her eyes.

Recognizing the signs of an imminent breakdown, Hailey stood quickly and pulled Allyson to her feet. "Come on. Let's get out of here." She steered Allyson from the table.

"Good idea," Allyson hiccup-sobbed.

Hailey put an arm around her and gently propelled her toward the long building on the west side of the pool, where the women's bungalows were. "Which number are you in?"

"Three."

Hailey guided her there, then pushed the door open so they could enter. Once inside she helped Allyson to the bed, where Allyson folded over on it, crying hysterically.

Now what? It seemed like giving Allyson her privacy was best, but Hailey felt bad just walking out on her. She looked around for a box of tissues and found two. Apparently guests were expected to cry a lot. Her thoughts flew to Gage. Had he cried at all over their breakup? He'd been almost clinically cold that day, the last time they'd spoken.

I can't marry you, Hailey. We don't suit.

She'd been too stunned to respond at first. Was this some kind of horrible joke one of her brothers-in-law had put Gage up to? *Don't suit?* What did that even mean? And who talked like that? *Not Gage.*

Allyson's loud sniffling jerked Hailey from her own problems to the present. She hurried over with the tissues. "Here." She pulled a bunch from the box and thrust them at Allyson.

"Thanks." More sniffling.

Muffled voices and footsteps came from outside. Hailey went to the window to close it and discovered it didn't close, not all the way, at least. Horizontal, louvered pieces of glass rotated down or up but did not lie completely flat. *So much for privacy.* She tilted the slats down as far as they could go, jerked the curtain closed, and turned toward Allyson.

Unsure what to do next, Hailey sat on the edge of the bed, intuition telling her that she should stay. If Allyson asked her to leave, she would. But it didn't seem right to sneak out now, when Allyson was so obviously distraught.

"May I see your ring?" Hailey asked.

Allyson held out her hand. Hailey took the solitaire and matching wedding band from her. "Is there a safe place you'd like me to put this? Somewhere out of sight, so you don't have to think about it every second, but also somewhere safe so it will make it home with you?"

"Unless I decide it's better off at the bottom of the ocean?" Allyson offered a tremulous smile as she sat up.

"Unless that," Hailey agreed. "Or maybe we should just

pawn our rings and go shopping. I've got a late flight the last day." She attempted a smile but felt sick inside at the actual thought of selling the ring Gage had given her. She'd rather it be at the bottom of the ocean than on someone else's finger.

"I can't do either." Allyson sighed, then blew her nose. "My ring belonged to my husband's grandmother. I suppose I ought to return it—to Brian's mother, not Brian."

Hailey handed the ring back. "What does *she* think of what her son has done?"

"Don't ask." Allyson flopped backward onto the colorful throw pillows topping the bedspread. "Basically it's my fault he strayed. I'm to blame for his unfaithfulness."

Double ouch. "In that case, you definitely ought to pawn that ring." Hailey exchanged a conspiratorial look with Allyson. "And send your mother-in-law the info and price for where it's at and what it'll cost her to get it back!"

"I like your thinking." Allyson smiled through her tears, and Hailey felt the slightest bit better herself. *There's always someone worse off than you.* How many times had her mother said that when she was growing up? It was true, though, and while Hailey certainly wasn't glad of it, wasn't at all happy for or about Allyson's misfortune, she felt the slightest bit better about hers. Gage's mom would never have blamed her for something he did. After Gage broke things off his mom had sent a sweet card expressing her sadness that their marriage was not to be.

Thinking of that now made Hailey's own eyes misty.

"This is the worst, isn't it?" Allyson said, her gaze catching Hailey's watery one.

"Yeah," Hailey agreed. "I mean, no. I thought it was, but then tonight . . ."

"You're right." Allyson pushed off the bed and walked to the mini fridge. She pulled out two of the bottles of juice that had come stocked in the refrigerators. Hailey had a similar assortment in her room.

Allyson passed one bottle to Hailey and kept one for herself. She twisted the cap off. "We have our health, and we have our parents—right?" She sounded suddenly uncertain, as if she'd just remembered she didn't know if Hailey actually had either.

"Right," Hailey echoed. "I have great parents and great health. So I guess what we're going through isn't quite the worst."

"Maybe not, but it's lousy enough to land us in Hawaii by ourselves for Christmas." Allyson leaned her head back and took a long drink.

"Hawaii for Christmas might not be so bad." Hailey stood and went to the window, then parted the curtain and adjusted the louvers slightly. Outside the moon had risen above the mountain behind the resort. Its light reflected in the water of the pool, and a slight breeze rippled the palm trees overhead. The earlier rain had ceased, and the air smelled fragrant and clean.

Hailey cranked the slats open a bit more and inhaled deeply, seeking the peace of their surroundings. "It is very beautiful here," she said softly. Then, looking over her shoulder, she added, "And a new friend makes everything better."

5

Pull of the Moon

GAGE SAT MOTIONLESS in the deck chair, hardly daring to breathe as he watched Hailey leave one room and make her way down the walkway to number five, what he guessed to be hers. He hadn't wanted to know that, to imagine her sleeping on the other side of that door. It was hard enough knowing she was here, within both reach and earshot. He had only to call out to her, or to touch her when they met again. But who knows—if he did call her name, would she stop? If his hand brushed hers, would she push him away? She had every right to, and he had no right to attempt either action. He'd made his decision—a noble one, he'd believed—though his mother hadn't agreed at all.

They'd barely been speaking when she'd handed him the envelope containing the voucher for this trip.

"I want you to go. You *need* this."

Gage had glanced at the price at the bottom. No way could she afford this on her fixed income. "Mom, why would you—"

"Because I'm mad at you, that's why." She folded her arms stubbornly. "I don't want you here for Christmas. I want you there, building houses or digging wells or whatever it is they'll have you doing, and getting some sense knocked into you."

He spent a few minutes, beneath her scrutiny, reading the fine print. "All right, I'll go," he announced at last, feeling absolutely no enthusiasm for the trip. But maybe it would be a good distraction. Then he could come back and start life over with the new year. *Without Hailey.*

It wasn't going to be much of a life.

Frustrated, Gage ran a hand through his hair. What he needed to be doing was finding a job at another firm. He couldn't exactly work with Hailey anymore, and he didn't feel right taking what clients they'd had with him. "I'll pay you back," he promised his mom, unsure when or how he would be able to. His savings were tied up with Hailey's in their business, and he wasn't about to ask for the money back. He wanted her to keep every penny. He hoped she was wildly successful, that at least some part of their plans for the future might still work out.

"It'll be good for you, you'll see." His mother's parting words echoed through Gage's mind. She'd said she didn't know about Hailey being here. *But what are the odds . . .*

He glanced toward Hailey's room and saw that she'd moved the slats of her window so they were open. She was brushing her hair, her gaze fixed on the moon above.

Still being careful not to move much, so as to keep out of her line of focus, he raised his own head to the night sky and found himself mesmerized by the low-lying clouds slowly moving across the moon's path.

The breeze had died down, and the trees were still now, but he could hear the tide rolling up on the shore just a short distance away, below the resort. The connection between moon and tide had always fascinated him. How could something nearly 240,000 miles away have so much control over something as magnificent and immense as the ocean?

It was one of nature's miracles that never ceased to amaze

him. He would never tire of standing on a beach watching the breakers roll in, just as he would never tire of watching Hailey, of being near her, listening to her, laughing with her, loving her. She could be thousands of miles away, and he'd still feel her magnetism.

She might as well have been thousands of miles away, for all his ability to do any of those things anymore. He'd forfeited those opportunities—and any right to her—for good reason. Or so he had to remind himself. Constantly.

But being here now, so close to her, Gage had to wonder. What force was at work, exerting itself over him and bringing them together again?

6

Thankful

ALONG WITH AN abundance of Kleenex and a mini fridge stocked with fruit drinks and other healthy alternatives to alcohol—no drowning one's sorrow in drink or illegal substances was a rule specifically listed in Hawaiian Holiday's charter—Hailey discovered that a smallish-size, hardbound notebook and a pen had been delivered to her room, left on the bedside table sometime during her absence.

She ignored her curiosity about the book until after she'd showered and changed into pajamas and was ready for bed. Once tucked beneath the lightweight comforter, and with both fluffy pillows at her back, Hailey reached for the book. A handwritten note on the first page explained its purpose in the simplest of terms.

It is not happy people who are thankful, but thankful people who are happy.

Gratitude for what you do *have is an important step in your journey.*

Begin your trek to gratitude and happiness tonight, and continue every day thereafter, by writing down five things you're grateful for each day.

The results will be miraculous.
Lucy

Hailey stared dubiously at the book, thinking of the times her mom had shared similar sentiments with her when she was growing up. *Could have saved a lot of money just listening to her instead of coming here.* Hailey smiled, imagining her mom's expression, if she could see Hailey—and this book—right now.

Suddenly her list was easy. Though she wasn't exactly feeling grateful for what she had, Hailey supposed being grateful for what she *didn't* have was a decent start. She uncapped the pen and began writing.

1. *I am grateful both of my parents are alive and that neither of them has cancer or any other serious illness.*
2. *I am grateful they are still happily married and our family intact.*
3. *I am grateful I don't have a life-threatening illness.*
4. *I am grateful my husband didn't cheat on me with my best friend.*

Hailey paused, the pen flipping impatiently between her fingers, as if it was eager to write the thought that had popped into her mind a minute ago, before all the others. Writing it seemed almost a confession—of the sorry state of her messed-up head and heart. But if she was being honest, she *was* grateful, had known it the second Gage stepped into the lanai tonight, in a sick and twisted and hopeless sort of way.

No one else was going to see this, right? She hoped it

wasn't supposed to be shared in any kind of group therapy or something. If so, she'd really be messed up.

She stared at the paper, at the line below the last one she'd written on. *Just admit it, already.*

    5.   *I am grateful Gage is here too.*

7

Charlie

"All right, what are we building today?" Hailey crouched in front of eight-year-old Charlie, her hands held out like she was hoping to receive a football. All she really wanted was a peek inside the folder clutched tightly in his arms. The other teams were already moving—going over instructions, picking up materials, and starting to assemble play equipment. Gage's team had started putting together whatever it was they were building.

Hailey told herself to stop noticing him and not to be jealous when he stood near Meghan, his partner for today, as they went over plans. But it was hard to keep her focus on her own team—she and Brock and wheelchair-bound Charlie—when, ten minutes after introductions, they remained at an awkward standstill. Brock, particularly, seemed to have checked out. He stood a few feet away, his nose in his phone, leaving Hailey to figure out how to get the ball rolling—or whatever it was they were supposed to be doing.

Charlie pressed the folder closer to his chest and grinned, revealing several gaps between his teeth where the grown-up ones hadn't quite come in yet. His brown eyes sparkled impishly.

"Oo-oh. I get it." Hailey straightened and glanced over at

Brock, her unfortunate draw for today's adventure. At breakfast this morning each of the women had chosen a piece of paper from a bowl. The name on the paper was the name of their partner for the day. Hailey hadn't been thrilled to see pool-boy Brock, as she'd come to think of him, on her slip of paper, but at least she hadn't chosen Gage. Just because she'd admitted to herself that she was thankful he was here didn't mean she was up to spending a day in close proximity to him. *Not yet.* But maybe—later in the week? What if it was more than crazy coincidence that they were both here?

"It's a game, isn't it?" she asked, turning back to Charlie. "You want us to guess what we're going to build."

His grin widened. Hailey couldn't help but smile back. He really was a cute kid, with a mop of dark, messy hair, expressive brown eyes, and that beautiful Samoan skin.

He was also going to be pretty limited in the ways he could help with whatever it was they were supposed to build, so instead of feeling annoyed by the delay, Hailey realized Charlie needed to have his fun and feel empowered where he could. Heaven knew the kid had a rough life.

From the presentation the previous evening, Hailey knew Charlie had lost both legs below the knees when he was three years old and part of his *house* had fallen on him. Charlie's life had been spared, thanks to one of the many nonprofits Lucy and Micah ran, and the generosity of a team of American doctors who had donated time and skills to his care. After his recovery, Charlie had ended up here at the orphanage near Laie, as his mother was unable to care for him.

It had all seemed so tragic last night, but the child grinning at her right now seemed anything but sad.

"Okay, then." Hailey rubbed her hands together. "I guess that we're going to build . . . a teeter totter that vaults kids off into a giant sponge pit."

Charlie laughed. "Nooo."

Loving the sound of his laughter and caring less and less that they hadn't started yet, she came up with another outlandish guess. "Or maybe . . . a merry-go-round that goes so fast all the kids throw up when they ride it?"

He hung his head to the side with his tongue out, making a goofy, sick face. It was her turn to laugh. The sound surprised her, and not just her. Gage happened to be walking by and glanced over, his expression as astonished as she felt.

Only the second day in Hawaii, and for the first time in over a month she'd found something to laugh about—even with Gage here. *A good sign.* Maybe Hawaiian Holidays *would* live up to all its hype.

Ignoring Gage, Hailey focused on Charlie, still flopped sideways, rolling his head around and making pathetic retching sounds. She decided right then and there that she adored this kid.

"Is he okay?" Brock edged cautiously closer, apparently deciding to join them again. He'd hardly shut up on the ride over, telling her about his condo in California, his job as an engineer, his gym, and everything else she'd never wanted to know; but since meeting Charlie, Brock had hardly spoken two words. Hailey had no time or use for moody men.

Gage was never like that. It was true, but she found herself resenting him all the same. He'd been perfectly normal—perfectly wonderful, even-keeled and good at communicating his feelings all eighteen months they'd dated. All the more reason for her to be furious at his last-minute change of mind. It had been so completely out of character. A car blindsiding her would have come with more warning than their breakup had.

"Charlie is perfectly fine," Hailey said. With a dozen nieces and nephews, she knew fake puking when she saw it.

"He's just mocking my idea of a vomit-inducing merry-go-round. Your turn to guess what he's hiding inside that folder." She nudged Brock with her foot when it appeared he might be about to check out again.

He stayed but wiped his palms on his pants and did that funny tic thing with his face that she'd noticed yesterday at the pool. She'd guessed he was nervous then, in spite of his swagger and boasting, but she wondered why he would feel that way now, in front of a little kid.

"How about a plan for a swing with an extra long chain that goes all the way around the bar?"

"Good guess." Hailey gave him an encouraging smile, laced with an unspoken threat. *Don't you dare think of abandoning me.* "Doesn't every kid dream of swinging high enough to go over the bar?"

"Wrong!" Charlie shouted, his mood flipping as swiftly to anger as Brock's had to sullen when they'd arrived.

Two moody males. Perfect.

"To swing you have to pump, and to pump you've got to have *legs.*" Charlie scowled.

Brock reeled back as if he'd been struck. He flashed Hailey a panicked look.

"In case you haven't noticed," Charlie continued. "Mine are gone."

"Oh, we noticed," Hailey said casually, catching an incredulous look from Brock as she silently prayed for the right words and approach to salvage the situation. "But I'm not really concerned with your legs. We were told you have a pretty awesome brain and had come up with an amazing idea for the playground. We figured a kid as smart as you could find a way to pump a swing—if you wanted to badly enough. But I guess that's not what's in your folder. Maybe there isn't anything in it, and we don't get to build any fun play equipment today." She turned away, catching a second, more pointed look from Brock, as if he couldn't quite believe what she'd just said.

Hailey motioned to him. "Come on, Brock. Let's go see who else we can help."

"Wait! There is something." Faster than she would have believed possible, Charlie wheeled his chair into her path and held the folder out. "I designed a chair coaster. Just an ordinary bridge or walkway for anyone else who plays on it, but for those of us in wheelchairs it will be sort of like a roller coaster. The momentum from the first drop will carry us to the second; then that will propel us to the third, and so on."

Hailey took the folder, opened it, and unfolded a significant-sized and professionally drawn plan, attached to which was a child's crude drawing and a sheet of notes. Brock came up behind her, peering over her shoulder. After a minute he gave a low whistle.

"You think of this yourself?" he asked Charlie.

"Yeah. After I asked the other kids in wheelchairs what they most wished they could do. It was sort of split fifty-fifty. Some really wanted to be able to swing, and some really wished they could slide. I was more in the slide camp, so I went with that." He wasn't quite smiling, but his anger seemed to have subsided.

"What's this?" Brock pointed to the plans and what appeared to be a ramp with a chain, almost like a drawbridge at the start of the coaster.

"Some of the kids aren't strong like me," Charlie explained. "Zane has cerebral palsy, and Kauri's arms are paralyzed, so they don't have the strength to get their chairs onto that first hill. This is a pulley system that will help them up it, plus it will control the speed that they go down all the hills. Some kids won't be able to go as fast as I will."

"This is pretty awesome—pretty incredible." Brock smiled for the first time since they'd arrived. "Some sweet engineering here. It's also gonna be a ton of work. We'd better get going."

Charlie nodded. "In case you're wondering, I'm really strong, even what's left of my legs. One of my jobs is going to be holding the extra bag of concrete for you on my lap. That way if you run out when you're mixing it, I'll have some right there for you."

"Very thoughtful." Hailey resisted the urge to ruffle his messy hair. "So is concrete first, boss?"

He shook his head. "Digging. We have to finish the holes for the posts that will hold the coaster. The last group dug most of them, but there are still a bunch left. *Then*, when the holes are finished, you get to pour the concrete."

"*We get* to pour," Hailey repeated. As if working with concrete was a great privilege. This kid was funny. *Digging—lovely.* She glanced at her fingernails and realized yet one more thing that not being engaged had changed. It didn't matter if she broke every one of her nails today. She wouldn't be holding a wedding bouquet any time soon. *Might as well get good and dirty.* "Let's do this."

8

Observations

HAILEY'S LAUGHTER CARRIED on the Hawaiian breeze and over the other voices and noises of hammers and drills. Silently chiding himself for his lack of willpower, Gage glanced over his shoulder yet again in time to see Hailey fling what appeared to be a handful of mud or wet concrete at Brock. The boy she was working with cheered and fist-bumped her before offering her shelter behind his wheelchair from Brock's payback.

Disheartened, and positive that Hailey's laughter was going to haunt him for the rest of his life, Gage returned to his work, screwing eye bolts into the low porch ceiling of the newly constructed playhouse. He might as well have been twisting them into his heart for as much as he was hurting inside.

Away from the moonlight and last night's moments of weakness, when he'd been reconsidering everything, his head was clear again—if not throbbing. This morning when he'd first heard Hailey laugh and had glanced over to see the source of her happiness, he'd never felt more certain that he had made the right choice breaking their engagement. But that didn't make giving her up any less painful.

He should have known it would be a child who was

responsible for the look of joy on Hailey's face. Gage had the feeling she'd been as surprised as he was at her laughter, and that had helped ease his hurt a little. *A very little.* He'd known at once when he saw her last night that Hailey hadn't recovered from their breakup anymore than he had. Otherwise she wouldn't be here, right?

That she'd given up the holiday with her family, that she'd left behind their "perfect loft above the store" and all her Christmas trappings and plans for events in the week leading up to Christmas told Gage that she, too, was still grieving what *should* have been.

If life hadn't thrown him such a curveball. He'd wanted to spare Hailey the same hit he'd taken but feared he'd dealt her a blow just as powerful.

Right now. But later? Five years down the road, when she held her newborn child in her arms, or ten years from now, when she cheered on a son or daughter at a soccer game, vaulted from her seat when her grade-schooler won the spelling bee, or got tears in her eyes during the Christmas pageant when her own angel starred as the angel . . . then she'd thank him for ending things. Well, if she ever found out why he'd done it.

If only she could see the bigger picture as he did. But of course he hadn't told her—couldn't have risked it then *or* now. It wasn't a position he wanted to put her in. She shouldn't have to choose something like that. *Should she?*

Had he taken the coward's way out, ending things before she could? Maybe part of it was that he didn't want to know the answer, didn't want to hear from her lips what the limits of her love were. Or used to be.

He could guess all too well what those limits were right now—slim to non-existent. She'd been shocked and hurt and furious last night when she'd discovered he was here. He'd seen it in her eyes. She probably hated him. And who could blame her? What would happen when the others here realized he was the one who'd broken their engagement? If the women had the same sort of introductions as the guys had last night, was it possible some of them already knew?

It didn't really matter what they thought or did. Hailey's feelings were the only ones he cared about, and he'd pulverized those. The best he could hope for here in Hawaii was that Brock or some other guy would help her start to put things back together again.

It was a lot to hope for.

"You ready for this?" Meghan, his partner for the day, held a chain out to him.

"Yep." Gage took it from her and fitted it through the hooks above, attaching a child-size swing on the child-size front porch of the prefab playhouse. After a ten-hour day it was nearing completion, and they were down to details. "Want to try it out, Aimee?"

"In a minute. Let me finish." Their six-year-old helper was busy poking bright-colored, plastic flowers into pre-drilled, and recently-enlarged, holes in the window boxes on the front of the house. Her brow was furrowed, her tongue poking out from between her lips as she concentrated on getting each stem in the right place.

Gage exchanged a smile with Meghan.

"Nice idea, partner." She high-fived him.

"My fianc—friend's—niece has Down Syndrome too. Fine motor skills can be frustrating for those kids."

"They can be frustrating for me." Meghan glanced at the roofline of the house and the screws that had given them trouble.

Gage leaned against the railing, waiting for Aimee to finish with the flowers. From the corner of his eye he watched as Hailey and Brock lifted a pole together, rested it on the arms of the wheelchair of the kid working with them, then began pushing the chair—pole, kid and all—running at what seemed a pretty reckless speed.

He couldn't tell what they were building. The first half of the day they'd been digging holes all over the place, from one end of the playground to the other. Then, for the past couple of hours they'd mixed and poured concrete and set posts of varying heights in those holes. Whatever they were doing, it looked a lot more labor intensive than the playhouse. It also looked like Hailey was having a lot more fun than he was.

Meghan was friendly, and Aimee was as sweet as they came, but there hadn't been a whole lot of laughter among them today. It had been pleasant, and Aimee's excitement at helping her new playhouse come together was infectious, but not the kind of magic that seemed to be happening across the way.

"Wishing you'd had a different project, or a different partner?" Meghan came over to the steps and sat down, her eyes following his gaze.

"Neither," Gage said honestly.

Meghan's brows rose. "Really? Could have fooled me. You've been watching them all day."

"Sorry. I didn't realize I was that obvious." Gage forced himself to turn his back on the scene.

"Not quite as obvious as you were last night at dinner. Hailey looked like she'd seen a ghost, and you looked like you wanted to crawl over the table and declare your love for her."

Gage gave a cynical laugh. "That would not have gone well—trust me."

"I'd like to. Why don't you do the same? Tell me your story. What's going on with you two, and why are you both here this week?"

Gage wasn't sure he was ready for therapy with anyone other than the program directors—even that wasn't high on his feel-good list. He shrugged and glanced at Aimee, still working her way through box number one.

"I'm not sure I'm supposed to say anything to anyone. Aren't we supposed to all have anonymity or something? The guys were told last night not to go prying into each other's business." Not that that was a problem for a bunch of guys.

"I'm not prying," Meghan said. "You don't have to tell me anything. It's just plain to see that there's something between you two, and it makes me sad to see people who ought to be together and aren't. Like my parents, each too stubborn and stupid to fix things—or to even try. Instead they're throwing away over thirty years together." She stood abruptly, swiping a hand across her cheek. "Sorry. It was supposed to be your turn to talk. I'm going to get the tools we left around back."

Meghan stalked off, leaving Gage feeling even worse than he had a few minutes ago. He hadn't meant to upset her. He just didn't want to talk about Hailey with anyone, especially a woman he'd met only this morning.

Hailey, on the other hand, didn't appear to have any qualms about jumping into a friendship with another guy. Gage took up watching her again, noting how close to her Brock stood as they wrestled another pole into place.

He wouldn't have pegged Brock as Hailey's type, and Gage had been certain she was annoyed with Brock this morning in the van on the way here, from her exasperated looks to her curt acknowledgment of his bragging statements. But now . . .

Something had changed. Since that first burst of laughter from her this morning, it appeared that they'd been having a good time together. Gage knew he ought to be glad. This was what Hailey needed—maybe not a guy like Brock, exactly, but to be noticed and appreciated and eventually loved by another man. *A good man.* A really *good man.*

Anyone less didn't deserve her.

9

Possibilities

"That massage was a little bit of heaven." Lisbeth stuck her toe in the water before shrugging off her terry robe and slipping into the hot tub with the others.

"I know, right?" Kirsten scooted over, making room on the bench.

"No need to move. I'm just going to sit on the step." Lisbeth settled there, instead of moving into the space Kirsten had vacated. "I shouldn't really be in water this hot right now."

Hailey and Allyson exchanged an uneasy glance.

She's the sick one? Hailey wasn't certain how old Lisbeth was, but likely at least a few years younger than she. With her blonde ponytail and the sprinkling of freckles across her face she could have easily passed for a teenager.

Childhood leukemia. And now a brain tumor...

"Do you want to talk about it?" Allyson asked in what Hailey had come to realize was her normal voice—soft and kind. Allyson would make a great therapist, and a great mother someday.

If her marriage hadn't fallen apart.

"I mean—if it would help to have someone listen," Allyson continued. "If not—I didn't mean to be nosy."

Lisbeth shrugged her slender shoulders. "There's not

much to tell. I have a tumor. Right here." She touched her index finger to the back right side of her head. "Doctors discovered it not quite two weeks ago. I got the last spot on this trip. Lucy always saves one for someone who needs it last minute."

"Shouldn't you be in a hospital or something?" Meghan bit her lip and looked uncomfortable. Not for the first time, Hailey thought to herself that Meghan seemed younger than the rest of them; or maybe it was that she liked to speak her mind. Several of the things out of her mouth the last day and a half had taken Hailey by surprise. It seemed Meghan hadn't yet acquired a politeness filter.

"I would have had surgery already, except for the holiday. My doctor doesn't actually know I'm so far from home right now. I'll probably get in trouble if she finds out." Lisbeth gave a nervous giggle.

"Nothing funny about a brain tumor," Meghan said darkly.

"We're glad you're here, and it's good to laugh," Allyson said in that calming way of hers. "Starting your treatment in good emotional health is important."

"But was it wise to be working like you were today?" Meghan wouldn't let it go.

Allyson flashed Lisbeth a look of sincere apology, as if she felt bad for starting this conversation in the first place.

"I didn't do too much today," Lisbeth said. "Darren and I put together teeter totters and installed swings. The frames were already up—the last Hawaiian Holidays group did that."

"I'd work another ten-hour day tomorrow if we could get that masseuse to return," Kirsten said, as if purposely trying to move the subject of conversation from Lisbeth.

"Here. Here," Hailey agreed, and raised her glass, clinking it with the others. Lisbeth flashed her a grateful smile, and

Hailey guessed she was glad to have the others, particularly Meghan, move on from the topic of brain tumors.

Hailey finished her pineapple juice, then set it on the side of the tub and sank deeper into the water, feeling more relaxed than she had in a long time. Working all day had been exhausting, the massage soothing, and this soak in warm water a final touch for what was sure to be a good night's sleep. She'd been without those so long that she found herself smiling in anticipation.

"What are you so happy about tonight?" Meghan asked. "Did the masseuse ask for your phone number or something?"

"No." Hailey threw her a questioning look. Meghan had been Gage's partner for the day. Had he said something to turn Meghan against her? "Why would you think that?"

Meghan shrugged. "I don't know. Maybe because you've already got two of the guys here wrapped around your finger."

"I don't know what you're talking about," Hailey said, her relaxation of a moment ago disrupted by a knot of tension forming in her stomach. What *had* Gage said?

"Sure you do. First you and Gage, and then today you and Brock were—"

"Leave her alone." Allyson moved swiftly, placing herself between Hailey and Meghan. "Remember what Lucy said, we're supposed to befriend each other, not accuse each other of who knows what. This isn't *The Bachelor.*"

"It's okay." Hailey stood and headed for the steps, intending to follow Lisbeth, who was already out of the water and halfway across the deck toward their rooms. But then she changed her mind. "I'd actually like to know what I'm accused of." Hailey faced Meghan. "If I've done something to offend you, please explain."

"It wasn't me," Meghan said with a roll of her eyes and a toss of her short hair. "And offended isn't the right word. Hurt is more like it. I'd say you hurt Gage today, the way you flirted with Brock."

Hailey's mouth opened in a surprised gasp. "I wasn't flirting. Brock and I were working hard—and making it as fun as possible for Charlie. As for Gage—he's the king of hurting people. Nothing I could say to him can compare with what he did a month ago." Her mouth snapped shut abruptly. Had she really just said that? Given the way everyone was staring at her, she guessed she had.

"Husband or fiancé?" Kirsten asked softly. She brushed aside wet bangs and looked intently at Hailey.

"Fiancé," Hailey said, shoulders slumping. Her problem wasn't life threatening like Lisbeth's, but that didn't mean it didn't hurt or that she wanted to talk about it—about Gage—with everyone. Allyson understood, but she didn't think the others would. "We were supposed to be married this week." They all knew now.

"I'm the one whose husband left." Allyson put an arm around Hailey.

"I'm sorry." Meghan drew in a breath, then reached out, touching both Hailey's and Allyson's arms briefly. "I shouldn't have assumed—I didn't know. It's just that I watched Gage watching you all day, and I could see . . ."

"What?" *What did you see?* Hailey felt unnerved to think he'd been watching her. She didn't think she'd been flirting at all. She certainly wasn't interested in Brock that way, no matter how handsome he was or how much money he made as an engineer. Cocky California boy wasn't her type. But to an outsider, might it have appeared that she *was* interested? And if so, would Gage think she had been purposely flirting? *To prove I'm fine without him.*

"Hailey?" Kirsten waved a hand in front of Hailey's face. "You okay?"

"Yeah." Clearly she wasn't, if she had to overthink

everything like this. "What did you see?" she asked Meghan. "When you were watching Gage?"

Meghan hesitated, as if uncertain whether she should answer. Then her brow furrowed, and her expression grew determined. "A man who's in love with you."

Meghan is wrong. So wrong. She has to be. Hailey's spa slippers flopped across the deck as she left the pool area and headed toward her room. *So much for that good night's sleep.* Her mind was wide awake and churning—anything but relaxed. Why was Gage here, anyway? The only reason she could think of was that he really *was* sick. It was a possibility that had been haunting her since their breakup. He'd had some kind of cancer as an infant. But that was years ago, and he'd never relapsed. If anything, Gage had always seemed exceptionally healthy. But what if that wasn't the case anymore? What if something had happened and, like Lisbeth, he faced horrible odds and treatment?

It would be just like him to want to spare me the pain of watching him go through that—of losing him. Hurting me now to spare me later. So like Gage. Instead of making her angry, this infused her with hope. Maybe she hadn't lost him—yet. Maybe whatever it was, he would come through better than he thought. Maybe he could survive it with her at his side. *Love conquers all.*

What if Meghan was right? *What if he does still love me?*

Hailey's heart was already pounding when she saw the paper wedged in her doorjamb. She reached for it, fingers actually trembling, then pulled it out and unfolded it. In the dim light of the outdoor hallway her eyes scanned the familiar handwriting.

Meet me on the beach at 10? Please.

10

Not What You Think

NOT CARING IF she appeared overly eager, Hailey zipped up the front of her hoodie as she ran down the weathered steps leading to the beach. She'd been here briefly, yesterday after she arrived, but at nine fifty-seven p.m. it looked a lot different—a lot more spooky.

Hand wrapped around the keychain alarm in her pocket, Hailey tried to push her fear away and instead channel a romantic vibe. Minutes from now she could be in Gage's arms, kissing him on the beach. All would be explained. All would be—

"You came." Brock stepped into view as she made the turn three stairs from the bottom. He stood beside a palm tree, waiting for her to finish her descent, a relieved grin on his face. "I wasn't sure you would."

He *wrote the note?* Only the shock of seeing him here—instead of Gage—kept Hailey from blurting her disappointment. The imaginary bubble image of her and Gage embracing on the beach burst.

"I came." Her voice sounded unsteady, and her eyes stung. She glanced quickly in either direction, just in case . . . When no one else appeared, she knelt with the pretense of unbuckling her sandals. She could have easily slipped them off but needed a minute to compose herself. What were the odds that Brock's handwriting would be so similar to Gage's?

Similar to the odds that Gage would be here, too, this week? She wondered why she was surprised at all.

When she'd blinked back her tears, and shoved her disappointment and hurt deep down, she straightened to face Brock. "So, why the beach? I think it would be better to meet there." She inclined her head upward, toward the glow of lights coming from the main house of the resort.

Brock stuck his hands in his pockets and looked suddenly unsure of himself. "I can't really tell you anything there. I mean, we aren't supposed to seek each other out or anything."

"Exactly." Hailey folded her arms and stared at him, waiting. Though she'd taken off her shoes, she had no intention of setting so much as a toe on the sand beside him. "It's late. Please say what you want to say. It's been a long day."

"Especially for you, I'd guess," he said. "Stuck with me as your partner, I mean."

"You were fine as a partner," Hailey said, hoping her honesty wouldn't feed his already overinflated ego. "After you got over your sulking this morning, that is."

"I wasn't sulking. Not really."

He was doing it again, right now. "Don't worry about it. I get that not everyone is a morning person or excited about building a kids' playground."

"That's not it," Brock said. "It's not what you think."

"I'm too tired to think." Hailey eyed the steps with longing.

"I kind of froze when I saw Charlie. His wheelchair—it really got to me."

"Oh?" She hadn't expected to hear that. She didn't buy it, either. Was Brock trying to convince her he'd been overcome with emotion or something? *Another get-the-girl tactic?*

He turned away from her and looked out at the moonlit ocean. "I felt like I was seeing my future."

Huh? "Anticipating that the next California quake is going to collapse your condo and you'll have to have your legs amputated?" It was a flippant response to his statement, but he couldn't expect her to take him seriously, could he?

He did. She saw it in his eyes when he looked at her again. "No. Not that. But I've been told these aren't going to work much longer, that in the next year or so I can expect . . ." He glanced at his legs and kicked awkwardly at the sand before drawing in a shaky breath and continuing. "In September I was diagnosed with muscular dystrophy. I've seen what's in store for me. It's not pretty."

Muscular. Dystrophy. How could that be? Buff, tan, handsome, arrogant Brock couldn't be sick. Images of frail kids in wheelchairs during a telethon popped into her head. How could that be his future? Hailey searched for the right words—*any* word that might convey her apology and sympathy. But why should he believe *her* now?

"I came on this holiday because I wanted to have a good time while I still could. And I hoped—" He shrugged. "—I guess I hoped I might meet someone who could make me forget what's coming—for a few days, at least."

His humble confession explained volumes about his behavior yesterday and today—everything from his facial tick to his obvious flirting, to the numerous times he'd dropped things or stumbled today. The first time that had happened she'd assumed it was a ploy, to amuse Charlie or make him feel better about his limitations. After that she'd been annoyed with Brock, thinking the joke was old and Charlie would feel mocked. Now she realized Brock likely hadn't been teasing at all. As for his flirting . . . He didn't have the luxury of time, so why not be direct?

Hailey felt sad, yet oddly grateful, honored almost, that he had chosen her as his escape from reality. If only she'd known earlier. In the space of a few seconds her entire perspective had changed.

She also felt burdened with the knowledge of his illness and ashamed of her own unkindness. *I'm as bad as Meghan.*

Wishing she hadn't been so flippant, Hailey placed her hand on Brock's arm and stepped onto the sand. They started down the beach, no words between them, just walking, her light touch and his vulnerability connecting them.

She knew what it was to want to forget—in her case, what *wasn't* coming. But his was a whole different nightmare. One that wasn't going to end, or end well, at least. *At least Lisbeth has a chance to get better—doesn't she?* Muscular dystrophy patients knew from the beginning what their outcome would be.

"You really were a great partner today—aside from the fact that you ruined one of my favorite T-shirts." She pretended to punch Brock's bicep, finding it hard to believe that someone so physically fit was at war—a war he'd ultimately lose—with his body.

"If that was one of your favorite T-shirts, I need to take you shopping."

Hailey laughed. "That's probably true. I'm not that great with fashion. But if you wanted your condo decorated, I'd be your girl."

"You could be my girl anyway, for this week at least." He stopped walking and looked down at her with eyes widened in a hopeful, puppy-dog expression.

Hailey shook her head but gentled her words. "The thing is, Brock, I'm not up for a relationship right now. And I'm not a rule breaker. We're already pushing things being here alone like this. I don't want to mess up this program for either of us.

I'm not facing a health challenge like you and some of the others here, but I am recovering from a pretty severe emotional blow. I'm floundering, and I need every second of this week to get my head above the water again."

"A little beach romance *might* help you recover. You know, clear your head." The puppy-dog look switched to a practiced smolder Hailey found all too easy to resist.

"Uh-uh. Not happening, Casanova."

Brock shrugged. "Can't blame a guy for trying."

"No," Hailey agreed. "I can't. But will you agree to *stop* trying? I won't be your girlfriend or your fling this week, but I'd like to be your friend."

He considered a moment. "That your best offer?"

She nodded. "My *only* offer." She withdrew her hand from his arm and stuck it out for him to shake.

"Fine." Brock pumped it up and down once, then winced suddenly. A second later his face twitched. "You noticed that, didn't you? Even here where we don't have much light."

There was no point lying to spare his feelings. "I noticed yesterday. I thought you had a nervous tick."

"Great." Brock let go of her hand and used his to rub the back of his neck. "People I work with and my friends are all going to start noticing odd things about me. At first they may just look away quickly like you did."

"I did?" She hadn't realized.

He nodded. "A lot of people do—the nice ones, the ones who were taught it's impolite to stare."

"What *should* we do?" Hailey asked, her question sincere. This was something she hadn't ever considered before.

"That's the thing—I don't know." Brock threw his hands up. "How do you make a person *not* feel uncomfortable around someone?"

She didn't have an answer.

"I do know exactly what *is* going to happen," he continued. "One by one my friends, colleagues, clients—they're all going to stop associating with me because it will be so uncomfortable to be around me."

"You can't know that about all of them," Hailey protested.

"I think I can," Brock said grimly. "Because I'd do the same thing. I wouldn't want to be around me either. No one wants to be uncomfortable, to think that what's happening to me could happen to him."

He was right. She'd experienced that phenomenon herself, after Gage broke their engagement. Her friends, in particular, had found excuses to avoid her—at a time she needed them most. And some of her family members had acted awkward around her. One of her sisters had even hinted that Hailey *must* have done something to make Gage change his mind.

"Maybe if you talk to them the way you're talking to me," she said.

"Maybe." He didn't sound too hopeful. "Not everyone listens as well as you do."

This made her feel worse. How many unkind thoughts had she had about him yesterday and today? Hailey turned away from Brock and stared out at the water. The tide was low, but the ground was still damp where the water had been earlier. She dug her toe into the sand, thinking of how many times this past month she'd wanted to bury her head there—or stay at home under the covers and wallow, at least. *But I'll get better. Eventually this ache, the emptiness, will go away.*

Brock's aches and pains and problems would only get worse.

"You want to talk about why you're here?" he asked.

"No." Her troubles seemed so petty now. Still so immense to her, but when stacked against what others were going through...

"Fair enough. We probably ought to get back then. Unless you've changed your mind about having a passionate Hawaiian affair, that is." His brow arched hopefully. "In which case, I'd suggest we take advantage of this highly romantic setting."

Hailey snorted. "We shook on you dropping that subject. Have you forgotten already?"

He placed his hands on her shoulders. "I'm pretty sure memory loss is a condition of MD."

She ducked out of his grasp. "Pity the poor girl who falls for that one."

"You think one might?" Brock asked, perking up at the suggestion.

Hailey shook her head. *Hopeless.* She kept herself from saying it just in time. Muscular dystrophy was nothing to joke about. Unless—maybe that was the only way to endure. Silently she vowed to do all she could to make Brock laugh this week.

"Back off, dude. She's not interested in whatever you're offering." Gage caught his breath as he peered over a waist-high ulei hedge, rimming the cliff directly above Hailey. His heart pounded. Adrenaline pumped through him.

A second ago Hailey had ducked out of Brock's grasp and shook her head at him. Now they seemed to be at some sort of impasse, facing one another on the isolated beach.

"What are you thinking, being alone with that guy?" Gage mumbled, shaking his head, damp with perspiration from his trek over jagged rocks and locked gates, through thick brush and people's backyards as he'd followed Hailey from above, watching out for her. Guilt tore at him for writing the note. He hadn't intended to trick her, and maybe she wouldn't have come if she'd known Brock would be waiting for her.

Gage's heart had leapt with near joy just a short while ago, watching Hailey practically run down the path to the beach. He'd never known her to be particularly quick at getting ready to do anything, yet she'd reappeared at her door, changed from her swimsuit to shorts, T-shirt, sandals, and a hoodie, in a record-breaking two minutes.

So she *was* willing to talk to him. For all of five minutes Gage had felt so relieved. He had another chance to end things better, to at least stay her friend. His mind raced with what he must tell her—how to explain why he'd done what he'd done—without really explaining anything.

He'd followed her at a distance, needing every second to get his words right this time. But before he'd even had the chance to try, she had started down the beach with Brock.

Gage had never considered that Hailey would actually walk alone at night with a guy she'd just met, a guy who—just this morning—had been clearly getting on her nerves.

Had she believed the note *was* from Brock? Gage thought his handwriting was kind of unique, but maybe not. Hailey hadn't seemed too surprised to see Brock waiting at the bottom of the steps, but had knelt down to take off her shoes right away, as if she couldn't wait to start strolling the sand with him. What if, earlier in the day, they'd talked about a beach walk tonight? What if, during the day working together, Brock had somehow won her over, lulled her into trusting him?

Gage had seen Brock put the note in her door earlier this

evening, but he'd guessed—hoped—it was a long shot on Brock's part. Gage had hoped replacing it with his own somehow took Brock out of the equation. But apparently he wasn't that easy to get rid of.

Hailey took off suddenly, tearing down the beach. Brock bolted after her. Gage lunged forward, attempting to force the thick bush apart. The web of interwoven branches clutched at his gym shorts and his legs, snagging and stopping his progress.

"Hailey!" he shouted.

She slowed and looked back.

"No!" Gage yelled, cursing his stupidity. "Run!" *Don't stop.*

Brock extended his hand toward her, almost catching the hood of her jacket. She let out a shriek and took off again.

Gage surged forward and broke free, clearing the hedge and almost the cliff itself. Pebbles scattered beneath his feet, then disappeared down the side of the rock as he skidded to a halt.

He grabbed at the bush behind him and stepped back to safety. *Hailey's not safe.* She was still running, Brock in close pursuit behind.

Hugging the edge of the cliff, Gage side-stepped. His eyes strained to keep her in sight. He was losing her. "Run, Hailey! I'm coming."

His shout was caught up in the sounds of the approaching storm and sea. His cry would never reach her, and neither would he, shuffling along like this. Holding fast to the ulei, he took one step then jumped, using his hand to pull himself over the hedge. He cleared it—mostly—then took off running.

If Brock so much as touches her—

Savage barking sounded behind him. *Great.* He'd seen the Beware of Dog sign on his first pass through this yard, but he hadn't seen an animal to go with it. Gage ran harder, covering much more ground much faster than when he'd come this way the first time, all the while keeping sight of Hailey on the beach below.

He jumped another hedge and vaulted over a low chain link fence into the next backyard a second before the snarling beast could get him. Gage glanced back and saw the dog still following, midair in its leap over the fence—teeth barred, tongue extended, long ears flapping like some sort of demon wings.

"*What—*" Gage ran faster.

He caught sight of Hailey on the beach below, still outrunning Brock. From here it looked like she'd put more distance between them.

A patio light flickered on as Gage dashed past. Elvis Presley's *Blue Christmas* carried through the open window.

Black and blue—Brock's face if he—

"Get him, Grunt!"

The sound of fabric ripping coincided with his shorts vanishing. One second they were there, the next gone. A tug at his boxers came next. He grabbed the waistband holding them in place, then half turned, kicking at the dog. "Get out of here."

It released the boxers in favor of Gage's shin, sharp teeth piercing his flesh.

Gage shouted and kicked harder. He smacked the dog on the nose, then tried to pry its mouth away. The door of the house flew open, and a woman emerged, waving a baseball bat in the air menacingly. "Grunt's got one. Call the police, Mack."

Police. Good. They'd help Hailey—and him. With another smack across the dog's snout, Gage yanked his bloody leg free, then stumbled backwards. The beast jumped on top of him, two large paws pressing his chest into the damp grass. Foul dog breath enveloped Gage's face, and a long string of drool descended from the dog's mouth toward his own.

"What are you doing in my yard?" The woman's muumuu brushed his arm. She leaned forward, staring down at him.

"Get your dog off of me, and I'll get out of your yard."

A baseball bat waved in front of his face; then the tip of the handle came down to rest on the bridge of his nose. "He'll get off when the police get here. Don't think about moving, or I'll have him tear out your throat."

The dog growled menacingly, as if to validate the threat.

"There's a woman down there on the beach. She's in trouble." The end of the bat pressed down harder with each word he spoke. Gage didn't dare lift his hand to push it away for fear the dog would bite him again. "I was following her, to try to help."

His leg throbbed, and he could feel the trickle of blood down to his ankle. But Hailey could be in much worse trouble. "I'm telling the truth. Go see for yourself. *Please.*"

"I'm not going anywhere," the woman said. "I'll see from right here." She moved closer, raising up on her toes and leaning over him as she peered down at the beach. Her muumuu dragged across his cheek, then covered one eye. Gage shut it quickly and turned his face away to avoid seeing beneath her dress.

Good thing too. The back screen slammed open once more and a man, a very large Polynesian, started toward them. His hands formed into fists, swinging widely at his side as he strode across the lawn. "What kind of vermin you catch, Marge?"

"He claims he was following a woman in trouble on the

beach," Marge said. "But I don't see any woman alone down there."

"She's not alone," Gage said, his eyes glued to Mack. The guy's arms had to be the size of his own thighs—both of them together. "There's a man chasing her. She needs help. We need to send the police you called to find her."

"There are two people on the beach," Marge said. "Near the stairs. Talking. Looks pretty friendly to me."

Someone else to help Hailey? Gage's panic ebbed slightly. "Hailey has her hair in a ponytail. She's wearing a zip-up hoodie and—"

"Yep. That's her. She just leaned forward and gave the guy a hug. Now she's picking up a pair of sandals."

"She's not running? Away from him?"

"Nope." Marge stepped back, dragging her long dress with her.

"If you'll just let me make sure it's her," Gage said. "That she's really safe. We're friends, and—"

"Heard that one before. Or were you hoping to be more than friends, running around in your underwear like that?" Mack joined Marge and took the bat from her, relieving the pressure on Gage's nose. Together they stood over him.

Mack smacked the baseball bat in his hand. "Don't worry. You won't be lonely for long." His grin was anything but pleasant. "Officer Sumtra will take you in. He works the beat here, picking up vagrants who trespass—and have other problems." Mack glanced at Gage's bare legs and frowned.

"I'm not a vagrant, and your dog took my shorts. This isn't what you think."

"Sure looks like it." Mack squatted beside Gage, one hand coming up to pat the dog. "He's not our dog. Just patrols the whole bluff. We all feed him and take care of him. Good job, Grunt."

The dog made a sound in congruence with its name before its tongue came out even farther, releasing the drool that had been hovering over Gage's face. Gage closed his mouth just in time but still cringed as dog spit made contact with his lip.

A second drop hit his eye. Gage shuddered, then felt slightly better when he realized it was only a drop of rain. A second and third followed, and soon his face was being plastered by the fat drops.

"I'm going in." Marge lifted the hem of her muumuu to clear the wet grass and returned to the house.

The wail of a police siren filled the air. "Sumtra takes his job very seriously," Mack continued, grin widening. He stood and walked a few feet, then used the end of the bat to scoop Gage's torn shorts off the lawn. "He loves taking care of creepers like you."

11

Watching

STILL BREATHING HARD from her run, Hailey slipped on one sandal, then the other.

"Might have mentioned to me *before* that you ran cross country in high school." Brock leaned forward, hands on his knees as he tried to recover from their impromptu run.

"That was a decade ago, plus I was running on sand. If my coach would have seen this performance she'd have been bitterly disappointed." Hailey finished buckling her sandals, then stood on wobbly legs.

"I may call for a rematch later in the week. Something like chess that doesn't involve my failing legs." Brock gave her a look that said he was still all too interested. When he'd suggested they make a bet—and if she lost he got to kiss her—she'd agreed, on the condition that if *he* lost he couldn't ever pester her about kissing or being his girlfriend or anything else along those lines again. Then she'd challenged him right then to race.

It had probably been a bit risky, but she still ran a few miles a few times a week, and in all his bragging about his gym sessions, Brock had never once mentioned any kind of cardio or endurance training. She'd run hard, the motivation of getting him off her case pretty compelling.

"Sure. I'll play chess with you," she said. "But no more bets. We agreed. I've friend-zoned you. And don't go blaming your legs for losing that race. They aren't failing you yet."

"Checking out my legs, were you?" Brock teased.

Hailey rolled her eyes. "Are all California boys this obnoxious?"

His face fell. "Ouch."

"Well-deserved," Hailey said, showing him no mercy.

"Deserved," Brock grumped.

She laughed, and after a few seconds he did too. Confident now in her role as his friend only, she linked her hand through his arm as they started up the stairs. She really was exhausted—from her unplanned run and from the long day. She hadn't worked so hard since she and Gage had renovated the shop.

Gage. He was like a ghost haunting her. First she'd imagined that he'd written the note and wanted to meet her on the beach. Then she'd thought she heard him calling to her back there. If she didn't figure out how to deal with being in close proximity to him this week, she was going to be even more of a train wreck.

Realizing that Brock had started to lag behind, Hailey slowed her steps and glanced at him. He had to be exhausted too. As much as she was grateful to have drawn a firm line of friendship in sand between them, she felt the tiniest bit regretful that she'd told him no. He needed someone in his life. Someone who would be there for him and really understand.

"You know, you might want to consider some of the other women here this week—as potential friends, I mean," Hailey added quickly when Brock looked over in obvious interest. "One has a pretty serious health issue as well. You two might find you have a lot in common."

"You're not going to tell me who it is?"

"Nope." Hailey grinned. "Only that she is very nice, and she's been through a lot of health stuff already. It'll be good to keep you guessing. You'll just have to put yourself out there and get to know some of the others, so you can figure out who it is."

"I'm on it," Brock said. "Challenge accepted—since you're a no-go for beach romance. Give me twenty-four hours, and I'll know who the mystery woman is."

Hailey laughed. "You do that. Only this time, don't try to impress her with stats about your job and your money. Be honest with her—like you were tonight with me."

"That is a billion times harder than you think," he admitted. "No guy wants to start off a relationship by telling a girl he's sick. I worried all evening. What if you didn't come? And if you did, what was I supposed to say? How could I explain my actions this morning and—everything else? MD isn't exactly a selling point."

"You did great," Hailey reassured him. "I like honest Brock much better than braggy Brock who sat next to me in the van this morning."

He winced, then stopped on the landing halfway up. "That bad, huh?"

"Worse." She grinned. "I was ready to ask the driver to let me off so I could walk."

"I'm sorry." His mouth turned down, looking contrite.

"You should be," Hailey said, still showing no sympathy. She was just guessing, but she didn't think that would really help. He needed a friend who would be honest with him. One whom he could tell anything to and know that he'd get a genuine response. "You should also be sorry for not telling Charlie why you kept dropping things and stumbling today. What if he thought you were somehow making fun of him?"

Brock's frown deepened. "I hadn't thought of that. Do you think I should tell him when we go back?"

"Absolutely."

"All right," Brock agreed. "I guess I could do that. He was a pretty cool kid."

They continued up the steps, their small talk masking the real reason for this moonlit walk. Brock needed a friend now and in the coming months, someone to help him get through this and to stand by him as he changed. Between the lines of their conversation Hailey realized he didn't have anyone in California who could be that person for him. Even worse, he *was* likely to eventually lose both his employment and the acquaintances he did have as his disease progressed.

"I'm scared," he admitted sometime later, when they'd reached the top of the bluff. "As much or more of living incapacitated than I am of dying. Seeing Charlie in that wheelchair today really brought that home."

"There will still be things you can do, even after you're in a wheelchair. Does Charlie seem incapacitated to you?" Hailey asked.

Brock seemed to consider her question. "Not incapacitated. But he also can't do the things a regular kid can."

"True," she agreed. "But in some ways he can do more. I saw how impressed you were with his design for the wheelchair coaster. Not every eight-year-old could come up with something like that."

"I suppose you're right," Brock admitted.

"*Suppose?* Don't you know the woman is always right?" She gave him a playful punch, then shrank back as he winced. "I'm so sorry. Did I hurt you?"

"Yeah." Brock made a show of rubbing his sore arm. "My muscles have been screaming at me since about ten o'clock this morning. I'm likely to be a mess tomorrow. Lucy scheduled an extra massage for me first thing in the morning."

"Lucky," Hailey said, a slow smile forming as she remembered how amazing her own massage had felt tonight. "I'm sorry I hit you. And I wish you'd said something to me sooner. I could have carried more of the load today."

"You were already doing more than me, whether you realized it or not." Brock shook his head and frowned, as if disgusted by that.

"You should have asked Micah and Lucy for one of the easier projects," Hailey said. "I can't understand why they gave us the hardest one, when they know your condition."

"Because I asked them for it."

"You what?" Hailey stared at him, open-mouthed.

"I needed to do something hard this week—one last time before I can't anymore."

"Men." Hailey rolled her eyes. "Always out to prove something."

"What do you suppose that one's out to prove?" Brock angled his head to the side, looking across the street.

Hailey's insides fluttered as she followed his gaze toward the silhouette of a man, head and shoulders visible from the other side of a police car, staring at them, an unreadable expression on his face.

Gage.

"I noticed him following us earlier," Brock said. "Met him yesterday when I first got here. He seemed kind of interested in you too."

"He did?" Her pulse quickened. Brock was the second one to suggest such a thing to her today. *He was following us?* Maybe she hadn't imagined Gage calling out to her.

"Yeah." Frowning, Brock shifted his attention from Gage back to Hailey. "That was *not* a friend-zone question you just asked. What's he got that I don't?"

My heart.

"It's not like that," Hailey hurried to reassure him. She pulled her gaze from across the street and tried to focus on Brock and not hurting him. "We knew each other before this trip. It's kind of a weird coincidence we're both here. That's all." How long had Gage been there? *Watching us?* Too late she realized how this must appear—she and Brock alone here, their nearness, their laughter and easy banter. She wished Gage would come over, that he'd give her the chance to explain. But when she looked over again, the police car was gone and he'd disappeared.

Wait. Come back. She looked up and down the street but didn't see him.

It's not what you think.

Twenty minutes later, when her head finally hit the pillow, her mind was still going full speed, overflowing with the many events of the long day. Before turning out the light Hailey picked up the notebook and pen. Maybe expressing gratitude would calm her enough that she could get some much-needed sleep.

1. *I'm grateful to have all my limbs.*
2. *I'm grateful to have met Charlie, who does not.*

Hailey smiled, thinking of him and his good humor that had made their day so enjoyable.

Last night she'd felt depressed when she heard his story. It still made her sad, but now that she'd met Charlie, she felt grateful to know that his life wasn't terrible. It certainly wasn't perfect, but he did have people who loved him, and he lived in a beautiful, happy place.

3. *I'm grateful I have good health.*
4. *I'm grateful to have met Brock, who does not.*

What a range of extremes she'd traveled as far as Brock was concerned. This morning she'd wanted to strangle him. Now she felt an almost sisterly affection and a genuine concern about his future. What could she do to make it better, or at least bearable for him? Hailey promised herself she'd talk to Lucy about that sometime this week. No doubt she'd have something helpful to share.

One more to go. Hailey nibbled the end of the pen. Just like yesterday, she was grateful Gage was here too. But it was more than that—more creepy perhaps, or more pathetic, depending on how she looked at it. More desperate. *More hopeful.* Something she hadn't felt in weeks. She touched the pen to the paper with brutal honesty.

5. *I'm grateful Gage is here, and (I think) grateful he was watching me today.*

12

Arrested Development

GAGE KICKED OFF his shoes and scooted onto the hospital bed, waiting for the doctor to return. He thought about what he'd seen tonight, about Brock and Hailey together a while ago, acting as if they were a couple.

It hurt. More than he'd been hurting already. And he hated that. But he wanted her to be happy, didn't he? And that meant he had to let her go.

Hanging on certainly wasn't getting him anywhere—except booked into jail after he was done here.

A stern, matronly nurse pulled back the curtain and entered the cubicle. Her eyes, already stretched tight by the severe bun on top of her head, zeroed in on him.

Sizing up the criminal. "I'm not dangerous." Gage gave her the best smile he could muster, considering the circumstances. Her mouth didn't budge from its stern line. Just outside the curtain Gage saw Officer Sumtra, standing guard, waiting for him.

As if I could escape with this leg. He grimaced as the nurse began to probe at his shredded flesh. She poured a liberal amount of some liquid on a swathe of gauze and pressed it to his leg. *Fire!* Gage nearly leapt off the table.

"Has to be sterilized," she said.

"Right." An actual torch might have felt better. He clenched his teeth and breathed through his nose until she'd finished. He dared a look down again and saw his flesh looked even redder and angrier than before. Great souvenir he was going to be taking home with him. He'd never forget this night.

"So, had a bit of a run in with a dog, I hear." The doctor looked up from his chart as he approached. His brow furrowed. "From the look of you, you're lucky to have made it out alive."

"Yeah. You could say that." Gage glanced at his grass-stained shirt, filthy arms, and the remains of his torn shorts, which Officer Sumtra had been decent enough to return to him, instead of keeping them for evidence. Gage wondered briefly if they'd allow him to shower before being booked into jail.

"It's unknown whether or not the animal that bit him is current on vaccinations," the nurse said matter-of-factly.

"A rabies shot as well, then," the doctor said, pulling up a stool near a tray of needles and other torturous-looking instruments. "We'll give you your first dose tonight, then you'll need to return for another dose on the third day after exposure, then the seventh and fourteenth days as well."

"I'm not planning to be in Hawaii that long," Gage said. What were the chances that he could find a flight home tomorrow?

"Your plans may change." As if doubting his ability to leave, the nurse glanced over her shoulder at Officer Sumtra.

"You can finish the shots at home," the doctor said. "You'll just want to make certain you do that. We'll also need to give you what's called Rabies Immune Globulin tonight. That one's not a lot of fun—has to be injected at the site of the wound mostly."

"Great." Gage laid his head back and closed his eyes. Why had he ever written that note? Or why hadn't he just met Hailey himself tonight, before she even walked down to the beach? And the even-bigger question—why had he broken up with her in the first place? He'd been telling himself over and over it was because he loved her and she deserved more than he could give her. All that was true, but he still couldn't help but feel he'd done everything wrong—and continued to make it all worse.

"Hey, Micah." Officer Sumtra's voice carried past the thin curtain into the room.

Gage opened his eyes and watched as the two clasped hands.

"What are you doing here?" Sumtra asked.

"Guest of ours had a little trouble tonight." Micah sounded amused, rather than upset, much to Gage's relief. He'd dreaded making that call, yet known he had to, unless he wanted to spend Christmas in jail. Though he hadn't done anything, other than trespassing and providing a snack for the neighborhood dog, it seemed likely that Mack and Marge would press charges against him.

"He's one of yours?" Sumtra pushed back the curtain the rest of the way.

Gage waved, then winced as the nurse injected the needle into his leg.

"Good to see you, Micah," the doctor said. He turned back to Gage. "Don't worry. We'll have you numb in no time."

"It's tomorrow you'll really feel it," the nurse said, a hint of glee in her voice.

Micah came over to the bed. "So . . . you went for a walk on the beach?"

"That's what I should have done," Gage said. "That was my intention. But I stayed up above. On the bluff—where the dog lives," he added. "I was trying to keep an eye on another one of your guests, to make sure she was safe."

"Hailey?" Micah grinned.

"Yeah." Gage sighed. "I told you this was a bad idea. I should have left the minute I saw her." Yesterday, as soon as he'd realized Hailey was here too, he'd spoken to Micah and Lucy. After explaining the situation, Gage had felt certain they would agree it was best he leave the program. But they had insisted it could still be a good week for both him and Hailey and that they wanted him to stay.

Micah placed a hand on Gage's shoulder. "You're exactly where you're supposed to be—well, maybe not here, and certainly not in jail." He shot a look at Sumtra. "About those charges . . ."

Sumtra relaxed his stance. "If you'll vouch for this guy and see that he doesn't wander too far in the next couple of days, I'll see what I can do."

"You have my word." Micah shook Sumtra's hand. "Thanks, my friend."

"Anything for you and Lucy," Sumtra said as he left.

Micah turned back to Gage and rubbed his hands together. "All right. That's one problem taken care of, provided your trespassing days are truly over." He pulled a chair up close to the bed. "Let's talk about what can be done to fix the bigger issue."

"Having a bum leg the rest of this trip?" Gage turned his head aside as the first stitch went in.

"Legs heal pretty quickly," Micah said. "Hearts, on the other hand, can be another matter. But we've got most of the week left, and I'm confident that we can send both you and Hailey home feeling a lot better than you do now."

"From what I witnessed tonight, I don't think she's feeling all that bad." Gage brought a hand to his chest and rubbed. His heart really did hurt. "It was one thing to give her up, but I don't think I can stand by and watch her be involved with another guy."

Micah leaned back in the chair. "She's not."

"If a romantic walk on the beach doesn't point to involvement, I'm not sure what does," Gage said.

"It wasn't romantic," Micah said. "Trust me on that. I'm not at liberty to tell you everything, but suffice it to say that what you witnessed wasn't Hailey trying to get away from a predator, nor was it the two of them playing some kind of romantic tag."

"Could have fooled me," Gage mumbled. "In fact, they did."

"You were being noble."

"And look where it got me." Though he couldn't feel the needle, Gage grimaced as another stitch went in.

Micah propped one leg up over the other and stretched, apparently in no hurry to leave. "Brock *was* coming onto her. You were right about that. But—according to him—she was having none of it. He suggested they make a bet—if he won, he got to kiss Hailey. If she won, he had to knock off any romantic advances. Period. Hailey agreed to the terms and chose a race as their wager."

"She's a runner." Gage felt himself smiling in spite of his lousy circumstances.

Micah nodded slowly. "*And* Brock has muscular dystrophy. He'd just told her that. It was the whole reason for their walk tonight." He shook his head. "No mercy, that woman. Which, of course, is exactly what Brock needs. Unfortunately, her lack of pity only makes her all the more attractive to him."

"Great." Gage's scowl returned.

"Not to worry. He won't bother her again. Lucy and I had

a talk with him tonight. Brock's pushed himself so much today that he's going to have enough on his plate just keeping up with the regular activities the rest of the week. I doubt he'll even think about going down those stairs to the beach again."

Muscular dystrophy. Of the four other guys on this trip, Gage would have guessed Brock would be the last one to have a debilitating disease like that. Instead, last night when Micah had shared the guys' bios, keeping everyone's anonymous, of course, Gage had pegged Brock as the guy who'd been a workaholic and lost his wife and baby daughter as a result. Brock was so full of himself, it just seemed to fit. *Apparently not.*

Gage couldn't feel bad about Hailey being hard on the guy, but he did think about how awful it would be to get news like that—to learn that in the future your body was no longer going to be yours to control, that no matter what you did, it was going to be a downhill journey.

He felt a strange empathy with Brock, though he doubted they'd ever discuss it. Guys didn't do bonding like that. But Gage knew what it was to have choices about his future taken away, and to have a body he'd counted on fail him.

13

Tough Shells and Thick Skins

THIS HAD TO be the worst holiday in Hawaii anyone ever had. For the second day in a row, Hailey was up before the sun. Now she sat on a dock, life jacket threatening to strangle her, knees pulled to her chest for warmth. She'd learned something about Hawaii. December mornings were chilly here too.

It didn't help that a light rain drizzled down on them, or that her muscles protested loudly with even the slightest move. Hailey glanced in Brock's direction, worried about how he was faring. He'd had to have been up at 4 a.m. to get a massage before they left. What kind of holiday was that?

At the core of her grumpiness was guilt. Instead of the great sleep she'd anticipated, she'd tossed and turned all night, worrying over what Gage had thought when he'd seen her at the beach with Brock. She wanted to explain what had happened—or *not* happened—this morning. Not that she really owed Gage any kind of explanation after the way he'd broken their engagement. But if there was any chance he really did care for her still, and that he was here trying to make amends and fix things between them, she didn't want to be the one to blow it. She wanted him back.

Her heart had known it from the first moment she saw him at dinner. Her brain may have taken a little longer to recognize the truth, but there it was. She couldn't be mad at him, because she still loved him so much. More than that, she knew him well. Gage wouldn't have acted as he did that night in the park, wouldn't have broken her heart and walked away, without good reason—or what he likely believed was a good reason.

But now Hailey feared he might be gone for good. He hadn't piled into the van this morning with everyone else, hadn't shown up at the dock yet. Lucy wasn't around to ask about his whereabouts, and Hailey wasn't sure she felt comfortable asking anyone else. Micah seemed the most likely to know, but he was busy running things, passing out life vests and giving instructions.

"Today we're going to be assisting the National Oceanic and Atmospheric Administration, NOAA, with keeping track of the green sea turtle population here in Kawela Bay." Micah's smile was wide, as if he'd just told a bunch of little kids they were headed to Disney World for the first time.

"Our naturalist guides monitor the turtles for their size, gender, location, and behavior. We're a little short on personnel this week—some guides wanted to go to the mainland for Christmas, can you imagine?"

Polite laughter followed this remark, but if his joke had fallen flat, Micah didn't seem to notice.

"This is where we come in. As we kayak in the bay this morning, be on the lookout for turtles. When you see one, raise the flag on your kayak, try to keep a safe distance from the turtle, so as not to alarm it, and a guide will join you as quickly as possible. NOAA is already familiar with most of the turtles who live here. Chances are they'll be able to identify yours. Occasionally we get a newcomer, and that's even more exciting. Even if you spot a turtle we're familiar with, know that you're a valuable part of this research effort. Green sea turtles are endangered, so keeping track of our population here is very important."

With skepticism Hailey eyed the kayaks clustered on the opposite side of the dock. Who had thought it would be a good idea to kayak first thing this morning, after yesterday's grueling projects? She'd hardly been able to raise her arms to put her shirt on this morning. Paddling a kayak seemed out of the question. She hoped those turtles weren't too far out into the bay.

After some additional instructions from Mark, one of the two NOAA guides who would be accompanying them, it was time to track turtles—or so the ever-enthusiastic Micah said. Mentally grumbling, and physically shivering, Hailey stood with the others, staying as near the end of the line as possible. The less time in the kayak the better.

"I'm placing my bets on Allyson," Brock whispered behind her.

Hailey turned to face him. "I knew you would." She smirked.

"My powers of deduction *are* superior," he said confidently.

"Hardly." Hailey rolled her eyes. "Allyson's the prettiest female here. I knew your shallow mind would choose to start there."

Brock's smug grin wilted. "So not Allyson, then? She isn't sick?"

Hailey shrugged. "I'm not saying. But either way she's a *friend* worth getting to know. She's really, really nice—much more compassionate than me."

"Isn't everyone?" Brock elbowed Hailey as he pushed past her. "Let me go in front of you so she doesn't get too much of a head start that I can't catch her."

"Be my guest." Hailey stepped aside, noting Brock's jerky movements. "How are you feeling today?"

He grimaced. "Like a truck hit me. Though after my massage it's only a regular truck, not an eighteen-wheeler."

"That's good—I suppose," she added.

"I'm better off than some people, anyhow. That other guy in our group, Gage, spent most of the night at the hospital."

"*What?*" Hailey grabbed Brock's sleeve as he turned away.

He shook his head without looking back. "Poor guy. Has it bad."

"Has *what* bad?" Hailey demanded.

"Not my place to say," Brock said. "Maybe ask him yourself."

Gage is still here, then. Hailey felt both relief and dread. The facts were adding up too quickly and in a direction she didn't want them to go. Gage had broken up with her a month ago, out of the blue and for no apparent reason. Now he was here in this program with a bunch of other people who had serious problems—many health-related. And he'd just spent the night at the hospital. Maybe the police car they'd seen last night had been for him—to get him there quickly.

No. No. No. Tears burned behind her eyes. What if whatever was wrong with Gage was life threatening?

She rubbed her hands up and down the sleeves of her windbreaker, telling herself to get it together and quit whining. If Gage was sick, she needed to be the strong one. She'd need to be positive—about everything.

Half this group had serious medical problems, yet they were here with smiles on, ready to do their part to preserve the green sea turtle population. At the least she ought to be able to do the same—and be happy about it.

Her resolve lasted about ten minutes, until it was her turn to step into a bright orange kayak. It wavered beneath her first foot—the foot she'd put all her weight on—and she toppled forward, heading straight for the water until a strong hand grabbed her arm and pulled her back.

"Thanks." Hailey looked up to see Gage's face inches from hers.

"You're welcome. Go ahead and get in. I'll keep hold of you until you're steady."

She nodded, or at least she thought she did. "You're here."

"Yep. Made it another day."

Was he joking or serious? Hailey couldn't tell if his smile was genuine or not. He did look really tired, with dark circles beneath his eyes. She remembered that just moments ago she'd wanted to talk to him, but now she couldn't seem to collect her thoughts. They'd scattered the second he touched her. Beneath his hand her skin sent a thousand hyper-sensitive signals to her brain, jamming every other logical thought.

Heart pounding, insides spinning in some bizarre combination of lovesick emotion, aching need, and wrenching loss, she somehow managed to slide herself into the kayak. Gage released her arm, and she mumbled another thanks without looking up at him. She couldn't, for fear he'd see the tears filling her eyes.

Her sore arms suddenly the least of her worries, Hailey thrust the paddle in just as Mark had instructed. She made good time across the bay, counting four dozen strokes before her burning shoulders forced her to stop. Glancing behind her, she noted that Gage was nowhere in sight. The rest of the group was also closer to the dock or the shore. Hailey rested the paddle across her lap and sat quietly, grateful for the serenity. Breathe in. Breathe out. *Pull yourself together.*

A peninsula jutting out from the island shaded the bay, blocking warmth from the rising sun. She wasn't as cold as she'd been earlier—vigorous paddling had helped—but the thought of resting in the sunlight was too much to resist. *Sunshine on my shoulder* . . . If only that was all it took to make her happy.

She picked up her paddle once more and slowly made her way to the tip of the peninsula, arriving just in time to see the sun burst through the clouds to the east. Rays of sunshine streaked from the heavens, reaching the lush land and blue waters in a spectacular display of nature. A rainbow formed before her eyes, arching from island to sea as well, the brilliant hues hovering magically in the air.

"No wonder you booked it out here."

Hailey didn't turn around to see who the intruder was. It wasn't Gage. Since he hadn't followed her, she would have preferred to be left alone to enjoy this moment but realized at once what a selfish thought that was. The bay and this morning were for everyone to enjoy.

"And here I thought you had the inside scoop on where all the turtles are." A kayak pulled up alongside hers.

"No scoop. Just a sunrise and perfect timing." Hailey pushed the brim of the hat covering her messy hair back to better see the newcomer. "I'm Hailey."

"Ray." He reached across the space between their kayaks to shake her hand.

"You're the seafood guy." She remembered thinking the platter he had carried the other night was pretty enormous and dwarfed him. "You carried the lobster."

"That's me. Lobster man." His ruddy complexion fit that description as well. "Don't get a whole lot of that where I'm from—Kansas City, that is."

"I've never been there," Hailey said.

"Good fried chicken," Ray said. "The kids and I get it about once a month."

"You have children?" Hailey asked, surprised. She hadn't realized that any of the guests this week had children.

"Not my own. Though some of them feel like it." Ray grinned broadly, a far-off look in his eye. "I feel kind of guilty not being with them this week. But my mom said she'd make sure they're all taken care of for Christmas."

At Hailey's vague nod and blank look he continued. "I did some time for drugs. Got out early on parole a year ago, with the agreement I'd do community service, teaching at-risk kids that drugs aren't the answer to their problems." He shrugged. "It's been the best year of my life. I'm starting school next month to be a social worker, and I'm going to keep volunteering. If I can help a kid avoid what I went through . . ."

"That's really great." Hailey smiled encouragingly, grateful for the surge of warmth his story infused into her beleaguered soul. She imagined he did do a lot of good, as open as he was about his past. "Do you mind if I ask why you're here in Hawaii? Most everyone else I've met in this program *hasn't* just had the best year of their lives." Maybe there had been a waiting list and this was the soonest Hawaiian Holidays had an opening. But that didn't seem likely. Not when she and some of the others has been able to sign up within the last couple of months.

Ray's smile grew. "My parents sent me—as a gift, to celebrate the way I've turned my life around."

"I love that," Hailey said. "What a wonderful story."

"It is. I'm one of the lucky ones. Where are you from?" Ray asked.

"Upstate New York." Hailey hesitated, not as eager to share her story as Ray had been to share his. And weren't they supposed to be looking for turtles?

"There's someone else here this week from there too." Ray snapped his fingers. "His name is—"

"Gage," Hailey said. No point in pretending she didn't already know.

"Yeah. That's it. You guys know each other before this trip?"

"Yes, actually." She didn't volunteer more than that. The conversation was heading toward uncomfortable at a rapid pace.

"Serious blow the poor guy had. I feel for him. That's got to be rough." Ray shook his head.

"Yeah . . ." Hailey pressed her lips together and nodded, as if she knew what he was talking about, all the while trying to figure out how she could discreetly ask.

"I'm gonna get going, but nice to meet you," Ray said. "I want to check out the snorkeling on the sandbar. Supposedly a lot of the turtles hang out there."

"Snorkeling?" Wasn't this supposed to be a kayak expedition?

"Didn't they give you a kit when you got your kayak?" He reached down between his legs and pulled up a mesh bag with snorkel gear. "Micah said in about an hour when the tide's a little farther out it'll be best. But I'm not that patient. I want to see some turtles now." Ray grinned, then held one end of his paddle up in farewell. "Nice to meet you," he called.

"You too. See you around." Hailey looked in the direction of the sunrise and rainbow and found the colors fading rapidly. *So much for that perfect moment.* And no, she didn't have the snorkeling kit. She'd been too eager to get away from Gage and the turmoil she felt around him.

She dipped her paddle back into the water and moved her kayak around a bit, doing a half-hearted search for turtles. What she really wanted was answers. Why was Gage here, and what was wrong with him? It sounded like something serious, something he ought to have some support for, from the woman he'd planned to marry.

✴ ✴ ✴

An hour and twenty minutes later about a half dozen flags had been raised. Hailey's wasn't one of them. She thought Allyson's kayak had a flag up, though it was hard to tell, as Brock's was practically stuck to its side. *Poor Allyson. Poor Brock.* Hailey wondered how long it would take for him to realize that Allyson wasn't suffering from any physical ailment—and that she was in no way interested in being his Hawaiian romance.

The morning mist had long since burned off, and the temperature had risen steadily for the past hour. Hailey had shed her windbreaker and leaned over to splash water on her arms frequently.

Right about now snorkeling sounded pretty good, but she hadn't returned to the dock for snorkel equipment. She didn't think her arms had it in them to paddle all the way back, then out to the sandbar again.

That doesn't mean I can't get in the water. Even wading would be refreshing. And her legs and back could use a break from being in this position. This decided, she began paddling again. Earlier, almost as soon as he'd left her, Ray had spotted a turtle near the sandbar. Both Mark and Micah had come over to verify, and there had been a lot of excited shouts from that direction. Apparently Ray had found a newcomer—cause for celebration, when a species was endangered.

But since then there hadn't been any turtle sightings out here, and that suited Hailey fine. No one was there now. She'd have it to herself, to enjoy a quick, refreshing dip.

At the dry end of the peninsula, where the land met the water before sloping down into the bay, Hailey awkwardly climbed from her kayak and dragged it up on shore. She stretched her stiff muscles, then stepped into the water, walking a good forty or so feet out with the level just above her knees. She glanced back to check on her kayak and experienced the odd sensation of being surrounded by water. She knew there was land beneath her, could both feel and see it; still, it seemed almost magical to be so far out here by herself, the water of the Pacific lapping on every side. She waded out a little farther. The ground sloped further beneath her feet, and the water level reached mid thigh now. *Far enough.*

She was contemplating sitting lower in the water and cooling off completely when something stirred a short distance in front of her. Mark's instructions and warnings before they'd started today flashed through her mind. If it was a turtle out there, she'd be fine, so long as she kept a reasonable distance and didn't attempt to touch it or alter its course.

Seals were a different matter. She needed to be at least 150 feet away and wasn't to make eye contact. They were aggressive and had been known to bite humans. *Was that a flipper?*

Hailey began to slowly edge back toward the shore, taking careful steps, her eyes scanning the water. Why had she come out here on her own? She could have cooled off right by the shore.

What if it she'd seen a shark? Mark had said they might see a hammerhead. *Or a dolphin or a whale.* She took comfort that at least it wasn't the latter, with the water this shallow.

It was just above her knees again, and Hailey's panicked thoughts were fading when the water a few feet in front of her moved once more. She froze in place, standing perfectly still as the ripples grew closer.

What to do? What will it do? Her life wasn't what she'd planned, but that didn't mean she wanted to be eaten by a shark.

There's no fin. Quit freaking out. Whatever it was hovered just below the surface, and the sun's angle being what it was, Hailey couldn't distinguish the creature as it approached. She pulled off her sunglasses as it grew closer, placing them on top of her baseball cap just as the form split, heading to either side of her.

Two of them! Whatever they were, they were big, and getting closer and closer and—

"Turtles!" Hailey exclaimed, breathless, as they came up on either side of her. They were massive, their flat shells giant and their fins long—so long the tip of one brushed her leg as it passed. Each turtle had to be close to five feet and weigh a lot more than she did, but their movements through the water were graceful. *Beautiful.*

She held perfectly still, only her eyes shifting as she looked down at them.

The turtle to her left moved more slowly, its head tilting to look up at her with an eye that seemed filled with wisdom. She felt hypnotized, as if she was looking back in time 150 million years. Hadn't Mark said these turtles were reptilian survivors from the age of dinosaurs? This one wasn't that old, of course. But much older than she, just the same. Decades older. The wrinkled folds on its neck and head were well earned.

Hailey forgot to be afraid. She wished she could touch them. They were magnificent—incredible, with their deep green shells and the intricate patterns covering their head and fins.

All too soon they were past. She turned to follow them as long as she could and found herself wishing she had snorkel gear after all.

"That was amazing! They came right up to you."

Hailey turned once more and found Gage standing on the shore near her. He was dressed in a T-shirt and sweats, instead of shorts or swim trunks, as everyone else was this morning. She hadn't noticed that earlier, when he'd helped her into the kayak. Maybe he'd come straight from the hospital. There wasn't another kayak visible near hers, but he'd made it over here, somehow. Had he walked all the way around from the dock?

"I saw you out here, and I thought you might need some sunscreen." He held a familiar tube out but made no move to enter the water to bring it to her.

"Thank you." Hailey waded the rest of the way to shore to take it from him. It was just like Gage to look out for her, particularly when it came to sunscreen and possible melanoma. His dad had died of cancer. *What if Gage has it too?*

Her fingers brushed his as he handed her the bottle.

More impulses to mess with her brain and heart. It was all she could do not to grab onto his hand and pull him close. "Thanks. That was really thoughtful."

"Looks like you're a little red already," he said.

"Probably. I was half asleep this morning when I put mine on."

"Well, be careful. You know how easily you burn. I wouldn't want you to feel lousy the rest of your vacation."

Vacation? Was that why he thought she was here? Did he think her parents sent her as a congratulations-on-not-getting-married-after-all gift?

The spark of irritation extinguished as quickly as it had lit. Hailey couldn't find it in herself to be angry with Gage. She loved him too much. Still. And he'd just done a kind, thoughtful thing. He'd always been like that, taking care of her more than she took care of herself sometimes.

Who is going to take care of you, Gage? "I heard you had a rough night," she said, hoping against hope that he'd open up to her.

"I'm good. Those turtles were incredible," Gage said, brushing off her comment. "And two of them! That must be the record for the day."

"I don't know about a record, but I'll never forget it." For the moment she dropped her questions about his health and why he'd been in the hospital, respecting the obvious, that he didn't want her to know. She could be patient and try a more subtle approach.

Hailey looked over her shoulder to the water where the turtles had been. That Gage had witnessed them, too, made the experience seem all the more special. "I'm glad you saw them." She found herself smiling at him, and when he returned her smile, she thought she might melt right there. *Oh, Gage. I've missed you.*

"Find anything over here?" Micah appeared around the tip of the peninsula, his strokes bringing his kayak closer.

"Hailey had two turtles stop by, swim right to her, one on either side."

"They were enormous." Hailey held her arms out to show him. "And beautiful."

Micah nodded. "Nothing quite like them, is there?"

"No." Hailey shook her head, wondering how she could have been less than excited about this excursion earlier this morning. Now she wanted to get back in her kayak and really try hard to find another one. And she wanted Gage beside her, glued to her side the way Brock had been stuck to Allyson's all morning.

"They're peaceful but fearless too," Micah said. "Thick skinned, strong. Years of swimming—sometimes against the current—has toughened them. They're tranquil, yet tough enough to take on just about anything."

"Oh, to be like a green sea turtle." Gage's mouth turned up in a half-smile, half-smirk.

Hailey pressed her lips together to keep from laughing.

"Ex-act-ly," Micah said, bobbing his head with the word and sounding every bit like the hippie naturalist he was. "We can learn a lot from nature."

Tranquil, yet tough. She liked that. A lot.

"That the turtles came right up to you is a good omen," Micah said.

"How so?" Gage began making his way farther up the shore, almost as if he were reluctant to get wet at all. *Odd. He's always enjoyed swimming before.* Hailey followed close behind, noting his subtle limp.

Micah paddled alongside them. "In the Hawaiian language the green sea turtles are called Honu—a symbol of good luck and longevity. To have two visit you—" Micah glanced at Hailey. "Well, you must be *very* lucky. The Honu is considered a sort of guardian spirit, and a navigator, the eternal link between man, the land, and the sea."

It sounded silly, yet Hailey understood what he was talking about. She'd felt something almost magical, some connection with the turtles as they swam by and especially when the one had looked at her. They had touched not only her skin, but her soul as well. She stopped walking, inhaled a deep breath of fresh Hawaiian air, and looked back at the ocean.

This. This was the kind of life-altering experience she'd hoped for on this trip—to find something so astounding and beautiful that she was reminded of the good in the world and the possibilities that still lay ahead of her. All was not as lost as it had seemed these past weeks.

"Let me help you." Gage reached a hand down to her as they ascended the rocky shore line in a slightly different place than where she had entered the water.

"Thanks." It seemed natural to accept his hand, natural

that he should offer it. *Unnatural that he winced as he pulled me up.* She couldn't shake the feeling that something was really wrong with him. *Something I might not be able to fix.*

But they were together—for a few moments, anyway. Her spirits buoyed and sank at the same time. Life did have possibilities. Her future was yet bright.

If she could only have Gage in it.

14

The Most

HE'D WAITED TOO long to bring her the sunscreen. Hailey's cheeks and nose were rosy, and not from cold. Though she did seem a bit flushed with excitement as she shared her two-turtle encounter with the others at their table in the Kula Grille at Turtle Bay. Most of the group listened with rapt attention.

She did that to people—captured their attention without even trying or realizing she was doing it, like with Brock the other day. There had been five attractive women lounging by the pool, and—as if she had some magnetic pull—he'd homed in on Hailey.

Maybe it's her red hair.

Gage had wondered about this before. After all, it was what had first caught his attention, that day his boss had sent him to the design firm she worked at to get the files for a new office space they were building.

Hailey had been bent over a set of plans, her long, fiery hair sweeping the paper on the desk. He hadn't even seen her face or heard her voice, and he was mesmerized.

Today her hair wasn't quite as shiny or as smooth as it had appeared that spring afternoon. But he'd still noticed it—and noticed others had, too, even a few who weren't at their table—when she'd removed her baseball cap and pulled her ponytail loose.

Gage remembered other times her hair had looked like this—all windblown and more curly than she liked. Normally Hailey straightened her hair and it hung long and sleek, well past her shoulders. But when it got wet, or here in humid Hawaii, her natural curl took over. She was finger-combing it now, trying to casually work out the tangles as she regaled those at her end of the table with her morning's adventure.

From past experience Gage knew he could tame her curls faster than she could. It was tempting to rise from his chair, go stand behind hers, and do just that. But then, he found everything about Hailey tempting. Just touching her hand for a few brief seconds today had set him on fire—a pleasant kind of fire, completely unlike the flames still shooting up his leg.

Since touching her wasn't his privilege any longer, Gage allowed himself to revisit memory while he stared, unseeing, at the menu in front of him.

Niagara Falls, last May. In spite of their ponchos they'd both been drenched—and laughing—by the time they hiked back to the car. But what was the point in going to the falls if you didn't get close? They'd agreed on that beforehand, and it had been a glorious afternoon, with the sun shining, the falls thundering, and the spray on their faces—and everywhere else.

"I should just leave my poncho on until I get home. My hair is a disaster." Hailey had grimaced at her reflection in the car window.

"I'll help you tame it." Gage had opened her door for her, then helped her shrug out of the wet plastic.

When they were both inside the car he'd instructed her to face away from him while he ever-so-gently ran his fingers through her curling hair—a difficult task at first, then gradually easier as, piece by piece, he smoothed and separated. It must have taken fifteen minutes. After a few had passed, neither of them had spoken a word. Gradually, after she'd realized it wasn't going to hurt, Hailey's shoulders had relaxed, until she was leaning into him so far that Gage finally stopped and simply held her, his arms wrapped around her, their faces close, hearts beating fast. Somehow the simple act of untangling her hair had turned into an intimate moment neither had been prepared for. She trusted him. He cherished her. They loved each other.

I still love her. He worried he always would and that memories, like the one he'd just been lost in, were all he'd have of that kind of love to last him the rest of his life.

Gage wondered if Hailey's feelings for him had faded at all. For her sake, he hoped so. He deserved hatred and animosity from her, but thus far the closest he'd received was her shocked expression at dinner the first night. Since then their interactions had been cordial, if not a little disconcerting.

He'd wanted to sit by her at brunch and had the feeling Hailey desired the same. *All the more reason to stay away.* When they'd arrived he'd purposely excused himself to use the restroom, and when he returned all the seats around her had already filled in. Part of him wished she'd saved one. The more logical part of him knew that would be playing a dangerous game neither deserved or could probably handle. Breaking a woman's heart for good reason, to ultimately spare her more heartache, was one thing. Breaking it because he was selfish, wanted to be near her, wanted to pretend she was his a little longer, was another entirely. And completely unacceptable.

So he sulked quietly at the opposite end of the table.

Allyson sat on Hailey's right. Gage noticed the two had become fast friends. He wasn't quite certain who the woman on her left was—Lisbeth, maybe? Brock sat straight across from Hailey, staring at her with some odd combination of adoration and lust. Happily, it seemed Hailey was immune to both.

Gage didn't trust Brock, and he didn't think Hailey should either—even after what Micah had told him about the reason for and the result of their beach walk last night. It wasn't like Hailey to do something so impulsive and irresponsible. Gage wondered how much of this change in her behavior was his fault. How much had he messed her up, calling off their wedding and walking out of her life?

A month out from his rash decision, he realized he should have handled things much differently. How, exactly, still eluded him. If he'd trusted Hailey with the truth, it would have put her in an awful position. He loved her enough not to do that to her. From their very first date he'd wanted to give her everything and had set out to do just that.

It wasn't to be. And hanging on like this, stalking her as he had last night, was only making things worse. He had a physical reminder of that now too. Beneath the table he adjusted his stiff leg. The nurse had been right. It hurt worse today.

Watching Hailey helped take his mind off the pain—or *that* pain, at least. He still wanted to give her everything.

Gage half smiled, remembering the day they'd found what was supposed to have been their home together. He'd had a friend keeping an eye open for properties in downtown Chaumont with both a shop and housing above. When one had come available, Gage had arranged to view it that very day—only to find that Hailey had beaten him to it, by a few minutes. He hadn't quite surprised her as he'd hoped, but he'd forever remember that day as one of his top ten memories.

They'd stood together in the bay window of the master

bedroom upstairs, whispering quietly and attempting to look serious so the listing realtor would think they were debating about the property. It had been a silly game, keeping straight faces when they wanted to shout, they were both so happy. He remembered wanting to pick Hailey up and swing her around off her feet, he was so excited. When she'd whispered, in that sultry way of hers, where their bed would go in the room, all pretense was off. He'd not only swept her off her feet but kissed her soundly in front of the realtor.

Then Hailey had grabbed his hand and hauled him through the rest of the upstairs, showing him the other two rooms, where his office and a baby's nursery might be.

A nursery. Gage looked away quickly, pretending interest in the scene outside. It was good he had a seat at the end of the table, as far away from Hailey as possible. But it wasn't far enough to keep the memories and his longing for her at bay. Against his better judgment he angled his body so he could watch her again. She'd finished both her tale and fiddling with her hair and was studying the menu—while Ray studied her.

Gage scowled, just as he had when he'd seen Ray's kayak pull up alongside Hailey's earlier this morning. *She's taken, buddy.* Except that she wasn't. Not anymore. And it was his fault.

"You're doing it again," Meghan whispered.

Gage looked across the table at her.

"What?"

She leaned closer. "Staring at your *ex fiancée.*" Meghan's brows rose, and her mouth puckered as she gave him a disapproving look. "You might have mentioned who she was yesterday, before I made a fool of myself telling Hailey she'd hurt your feelings by flirting with Brock."

Gage resisted the urge to put his menu up as a barrier between them. "How was I to know you'd do something like that?" he asked through clenched teeth. Meghan was worse than his mom. *Maybe Mom knows her and sent her to do her dirty work.*

Before Meghan could come up with a proper retort—and Gage was sure she would—Darren returned from the restroom and took the seat beside her. He placed his order with the others, then launched into a conversation with Caleb, on his other side.

There's a guy who has a right to be sullen. Though they weren't necessarily supposed to know who was who with the problems that had led them all here, somehow most of that had been revealed already. It had happened in casual conversation, sentences dropped here or there. At dinner last night Gage had learned that Caleb's wife had left him and taken their baby girl with her. This, after the failure of his business and his having to declare bankruptcy—all of which Caleb was just figuring out didn't really matter, in comparison to losing his family. Too late he'd realized that during the past five years of his life, devoted almost entirely to his failed business, he'd had his priorities wrong.

My life could be worse.

"You're so dense," Meghan whispered.

Gage felt torn between defending himself and his actions and taking a vow of silence. If he didn't speak to Meghan the rest of the week, would she leave him alone?

Micah and Lucy had claimed the seats next to him on this side of the table but were busy elsewhere at the moment, arranging things for the next part of the day's itinerary. He willed them to hurry back so he wouldn't have to deal with Meghan. She'd been nice enough yesterday, but apparently that had changed. *What did Hailey tell her?*

"It's obvious you care for her," Meghan whispered.

He nodded.

"Then why—"

Gage met Meghan's challenging gaze with one of his own. "I can't give Hailey the life she deserves. I can't give her what she wants the most." *Let Meghan challenge that.*

She did.

"Men." She rolled her eyes.

"What?" he asked, then wished he hadn't.

"Has it *never* occurred to you?" Meghan's eyes scrunched as if her head pained her. "*You* are what she wants the most."

15

The Places You'll Go

LUCY MADE HER way around the lanai, handing white, sealed envelopes to each person. "In these envelopes you'll find two hundred fifty dollars of the money you paid to Hawaiian Holidays Inc. for this trip."

"No, we're not cancelling an excursion." Micah raised his hands high, as if to stop the questions before they came. "This is simply your Christmas spending money—that we budgeted for you." He grinned. "Lucy's idea."

Huh? Hailey shifted in her seat, suddenly uncomfortable. Were they supposed to get gifts for each other or something?

"Your Christmas spending money for the children at the orphanage," Lucy hurried to clarify with an eye roll Micah's direction. "Though he'd like you to think we want you to buy us presents."

Polite laughter filtered around the lanai, and Hailey breathed a sigh of relief. Shopping for kids she could do. Not a problem. While she was at it she could shop for her family. She'd been too depressed to do anything Christmas-related this past month, shopping included, and she didn't want to disappoint her nieces and nephews. She also wanted to get a few things for her new friends. A ring for Allyson to wear in place of her wedding band, a cute hat or scarf for Lisbeth to wear after her surgery and while she was going through chemo . . .

Lucy began handing out a second set of envelopes, these with individual names on the front. "Inside you'll find the name and wishes of the child to whom you've been assigned as a secret Santa. Some of you will have the same children you worked with yesterday. Others will be meeting the child they will be buying for shortly, when we head over to the orphanage for a couple hours of playtime."

Brock raised his hand. "When are we going to finish the playground? Charlie, Hailey, and I have quite a bit of work left to do on our project."

"Good question." Micah pushed off the table he'd been leaning against. "About half of your projects were finished yesterday, but there are several that still need completion. Tomorrow morning, bright and early—" he paused, an almost devious grin on his face—"we'll be heading back to the orphanage to finish those as well as tackle a few additional tasks—spreading playground bark and things like that. Don't worry. We've got plenty of work for all."

Part of Hailey wanted to groan—her sore shoulders and back, her stiff legs, her tired body. *Who'd have thought a week in Hawaii could be so unrelaxing?* But another part of her really wanted to see this playground complete, to witness Charlie ride the chair coaster he'd dreamed up and helped design.

"All right, everyone, to the van," Lucy said loudly, above the sound of envelopes being torn open and the murmur of conversation. "You can read about your child and his or her needs on the way. We have a little over two hours before we need to head to town for Christmas shopping."

"Never a dull moment," Kirsten said.

"Exactly." Lucy's head bobbed in agreement. "When

you're busy focusing on others and doing good, that doesn't leave a lot of time to dwell on your own problems."

"Healing by exhaustion," Meghan grumbled.

"No. Healing by doing good for others." Ray smiled at her. "It really does work. I'm living proof." He strode past them, hurrying toward the twelve-passenger van parked out front.

"Old Ray is just one bright ray of sunshine, isn't he?" Caleb asked, shaking his head, as if he couldn't quite understand how or why this was.

"Yes." Hailey quickened her steps, thinking that it would be pleasant to sit by Ray on the drive to the orphanage. "He is. He hit his rock bottom a long time ago, and he might just be the only one of us who has figured out how to get up again."

"Hello." Hailey pushed the squeaking door open. "Amura?" Brock had been assigned to be a secret Santa for Charlie, and she had been given another child, a little girl named Amura. Oddly, her paper hadn't said much else. Micah had said the little girl would be found down this hallway, inside the orphanage, whereas most of the other children had been waiting outside, eager to meet the "friends" who had come to play with them this afternoon. *What is her disability,* Hailey wondered, *that she's not outside too?*

In contrast with the happy voices and chatter outside, this part of the orphanage seemed too quiet, and almost gloomy, with its plain, unadorned walls and tile floor. Where was the children's artwork? Where were the pictures? *Shouldn't they have painted it something other than beige?*

Hailey felt her inner designer twitching with discomfort. If this long hall was indicative of the rest of the orphanage's décor, the place was in need of some serious help.

A door stood ajar at the end of the hallway, and Hailey called out another hello as she entered through it.

A girl who looked to be around ten years old rose to greet her.

"Amura?" Hailey smiled, noting the girl held a worn copy of *Little House on the Prairie*. What a different world that must seem, compared to life on this island.

"Amura is sleeping, but she should be awake soon." The girl glanced over her shoulder at a crib.

"A baby?" Hailey asked surprised. "I didn't know there were any infants here."

"Amura is the only one. She wasn't supposed to be here, but her mother is sick."

"I see." Hailey didn't, not really. Did the child not have a father? Or grandparents? Or aunts or uncles? Why would they let this baby girl be alone in an orphanage instead of at home, or at the least, with family? *Especially at Christmas.*

The older girl left, and Hailey made her way to the crib, where a too-thin, but beautiful baby slept. An abundance of dark curls covered her head, and she was smiling in her sleep.

"Oh, good. You found her." Lucy tiptoed into the room, a clipboard thick with loose papers in her hand. Her hair was windblown, as if she'd driven over here in an open-top jeep instead of the van, and for the first time Hailey noticed the dark circles beneath Lucy's eyes.

If I'm not getting enough sleep, she must not be getting any. All of these meals and activities, from the orphanage, to the masseuse, to kayaking with turtles, had to take some serious planning and coordination.

"Are you okay?" Hailey asked. Something about usually calm, collected Lucy seemed off.

"Just a bit flustered is all." Lucy ran a hand over her hair, as if just now aware of its state. She spoke softly. "You probably caught that your note about Amura was handwritten, instead of typed like the others. She was a last-minute addition to our sub-for-Santa list—not supposed to be here. But her mother died early this morning."

"Oh, no. How terrible." Hailey felt a rush of sadness as she looked down at the baby and searched for the right words. Once again she found herself at a loss. "What happens now?" she asked. "Will Amura's father or other relatives take care of her?"

Lucy shook her head sadly. "Her family is from the Sous Le Vent islands, some of the poorest in French Polynesia. With her medical condition they'll not be able to care for her. Amura's mother might have been trained to see to her needs, but her father must work, and her care would likely fall to a sibling."

"What is wrong with her?" Hailey looked down on the child, still sleeping peacefully, in spite of their conversation.

"She had a ventricular septal defect—she was born with a hole in her heart. One that, in her case, wasn't small enough it was likely to close on its own. She had surgery on the mainland two months ago, then returned to us this week. Her parents were supposed to have been here already and to have her home by Christmas." Lucy sighed sadly. "Not all stories have happy endings—or at least the ones we planned."

"So she'll stay here?" The orphanage didn't seem like a terrible place, yet it seemed like this little girl ought to have a family of her own. "Surely she could be adopted."

"Oh, she will." Lucy's face brightened. "We're working on that right now. We have a partnership with an adoption agency here and several others on the mainland. That's why there aren't too many permanent residents at the orphanage. Our goal is to find all of these children homes and, in the interim, to make this place as awesome as possible."

"The new playground," Hailey said.

"Yes. I hope you don't feel used in this endeavor. Typically our Hawaiian Holiday participants get as much out or more out of their service at the orphanage as the kids do."

"No complaints here." Hailey attempted to roll her shoulders. "Well, maybe a few from my muscles."

Lucy laughed, and the baby stirred.

"See how she smiles, even in her sleep." Lucy bent over the crib. "That's what her name means—big smile. She's had a lot of them since she's been here."

"Even without her family and with being sick?" Hailey found herself wishing Amura would wake up so she could hold her and play with her.

"Even then. Though I believe she is feeling much better than she was before her surgery. She's still sleeping a lot as she recovers, but her heart is going to be just fine. The greatest worry now is endocarditis. Cleanliness has become extremely important, so she doesn't develop an infection. We have to be careful that her bottles are sterilized and that she doesn't get something in her mouth that she shouldn't."

"A tall order with a baby." Hailey thought of her sisters' children and the way they'd stuffed anything and everything into their mouths as babies. She felt slightly panicked at the thought of such a fragile child *here*. Not that the orphanage was a bad place, but hadn't a ten-year-old just been watching Amura?

"Good afternoon, sunshine," Lucy crooned.

Hailey looked down into a pair of the prettiest brown eyes she'd ever seen. The baby blinked and wiggled a little, one hand coming free of its light blanket. "What a beautiful baby."

Lucy reached down to pick Amura up. "Just wait until she's a little healthier and has filled out more. She'll be stunning." Without asking if Hailey wanted to hold Amura, Lucy placed the baby in her arms.

Holding a baby wasn't a new sensation, with all the nieces and nephews her siblings had produced. Hailey's arms cradled the little girl, then lifted her to her shoulder, where she'd found most babies preferred to be.

"How old is she?" Hailey asked. Amura still had that sweet baby smell, and her skin was delicate and soft.

"Almost six months," Lucy said, her voice wistful. "I'm sure she's going to make some lucky family very happy." She paused and seemed about to say something else, then abruptly turned to go. "I'll leave you two to get acquainted." Lucy slipped out of the room as Hailey settled into the rocker. She sat Amura on her lap, facing her, and was immediately rewarded with another bright smile.

Two tiny bottom teeth were barely visible inside Amura's mouth, and Hailey guessed more teeth were getting ready to make an appearance, from the way Amura chomped on her fist and the copious amount of drool making its way down her chin.

Hailey reached up to catch some of the dribble, and Amura giggled—a sound that seemed as magical as seeing the turtles had been, though in an entirely different way.

Here was a child, a baby, who had survived being born with a heart defect, being taken from her family and sent thousands of miles away, having open heart surgery, and now losing her mother. *So much for one so small.*

And yet she was smiling. That she was too young to fully understand any of these hardships didn't seem to matter. She would never remember her mother. Likely she would grow up not knowing the father and siblings she'd left behind.

Hailey gathered Amura close, holding her near to her own heart, running her hand over the baby's soft curls. She wanted to protect Amura from this hurt, wished she could have done something to help the child's mother, hoped that the woman who took her place would love this little girl so very much.

Amura wiggled against all this affection, clearly wanting something more entertaining than being held and rocked by an overly emotional woman.

Hailey looked around for something that might work as a baby toy.

Age-appropriate baby toys. She'd have fun shopping for those later this evening. As well as pajamas, dresses, little shoes, and hair accessories, a super soft quilt. Christmas shopping held new appeal. But for now—

The abandoned copy of *Little House on the Prairie* lay on top of a low bookcase. Hailey glanced among the titles, searching for something colorful, and found a Seuss. *Oh, the Places You'll Go!* seemed somehow fitting for a little girl who had traveled so far in her first months of life and had yet to travel more to meet the people who would become her family.

Hailey pulled the slender volume from the shelf, turned Amura around on her lap so that she could see the pictures, and began reading.

The Seuss lilt and rhyme were easy to get caught up in. Amura's legs churned happily, and Hailey found comfort in the story's familiar rhythm. She'd grown up in a house filled with books, including just about every volume of Dr. Seuss. Aloud she read about the heights one could reach, followed by bang-ups and hang-ups and lurches.

No kidding. She'd never found Seuss quite so brilliant before, but today he was spot on. Un-slumping oneself was neither fun nor easily done.

"You may even end up in Hawaii for Christmas."

Hailey and Amura both startled at the voice and looked up. Gage stood in the doorway, a wriggling toddler tucked beneath his arm like a football.

"On the same island as—" Gage's poetic ability seemed to fail him—"as someone you know," he finished—rather lamely, Hailey thought.

"Good thing I wasn't a children's book author." He stepped into the room.

"If you're asking if I knew you'd be here this week, I didn't." Hailey tracked his progress across the floor, her heart already pounding at his nearness.

"I wasn't asking. I could tell you were as surprised as I was." Gage carried the squirming toddler to the back of the room and deposited him beside a pile of giant Legos. "He belongs to one of the staff," he added, at her questioning look. "I volunteered to bring him inside, hoping I might find you here." Gage pulled up a stool opposite her and sat on it. "Can we talk a minute?"

She felt her eyes smart as they met his blue ones. "Sure." *Yes!* Her reply was barely audible, her vocal cords failing her at a crucial moment. She wanted to talk to Gage, but now her mind scrambled for the right words.

"Aren't you a beauty." Gage smiled at Amura and wiggled his fingers in front of her. Her little fist latched onto one and immediately began towing Gage's hand toward her mouth.

"Probably shouldn't let her do that," Hailey said, hating to disrupt their interaction. If playing with a baby would keep Gage here and talking . . . "Lucy said to be extra careful with what Amura puts in her mouth. She recently had open heart surgery, so the risk of infection is high."

Gage gave a low whistle. "Sounds pretty serious. So you're beautiful *and* strong." He spoke to Amura as he gently pulled his hand away. "Just like the lady who's holding you."

"Thanks," Hailey managed, her voice still soft.

"I'm not surprised they assigned you the baby." His smile

seemed sad. "You always were good with them—'Auntie Hailey will get him to sleep. Give the baby to her.'" His mimic of her sisters didn't seem rude, but truthful.

Hailey's uncertainty grew, and she looked away. How many times had her siblings said things like that, and in front of Gage? Had it somehow bothered him? She'd always believed he liked her big, crazy family. He'd said he did, having been an only child himself and having lost his father at fourteen. He'd also said he wanted a big family of his own. *Our own.* A life filled with kids and chaos. But that was so different from what he'd grown up with. Had he only pretended to embrace it? Had someone done something to scare him away?

"Did that bother you when I took care of my nieces or nephews?" Had she inadvertently neglected Gage in the process?

"No—not at all. Hailey—" He reached out, then drew his hands back, as if remembering he couldn't touch her anymore. "My breaking our engagement had nothing to do with anything you did or said."

"Then what—" Hailey set the book aside and shifted Amura farther back on her lap.

"I had some news . . ." He leaned forward, elbows braced on his knees, head down. "That changed everything."

"Did it change the way you felt about me?" she blurted, then hurried on, afraid of his answer. "Because the way I feel about you hasn't changed at all. I love you, Gage."

"You shouldn't. You won't—someday."

"*Why?*" Desperate to keep him here with her, and to reach him, Hailey took his hand, further disheartened when it lay limp in hers. "*What* is going on with you, Gage? Tell me. *Trust* me. You used to."

Still not looking at her, he shook his head. "It would be wrong of me. It wouldn't be fair."

"Let me decide what's fair," she said. "Because the most *un*fair thing that has ever happened to me was you breaking our engagement without any explanation at all. And saying 'we don't suit' does *not* count as an explanation." She was finding her voice now. "We suit perfectly, and you know it. We share the same dreams, we both love adventure. We enjoy the same books and movies. We make each other laugh. You make me want to be the best person I can—to try to be as good as you. We're like an old couple who've been together so long that they think alike and complete each other's sentences. That we both ended up here, in this program, at Christmas is proof." She squeezed his hand, still hoping for a response.

"Even our careers match. Architects and designers go together like peanut butter and jelly. Or bread and butter, at least. You're the bread, and I'm the butter for now. But the business is going to take off. I know it will, Gage. I thought you did too. I know purchasing the house was a risk, but I thought you believed in me—in us. In our dreams."

"I did—I do. This isn't about the business or the house or anything to do with money. It has everything to do with how much I care about you, and your dreams."

"Our dreams," Hailey said.

He shook his head. "They can't be. Not anymore. On the way home from Thanksgiving I had a conversation with my mom, and . . ."

And? Hailey waited, but he didn't continue. Gage only had his mom. He would be devastated if something happened to his only remaining parent. Hailey had asked him before if something was wrong with his mom, and he'd said no, but maybe whatever was wrong had been too new then, too recent and he'd been unable to talk about it. "Is she sick? Did she have another stroke?"

Gage shook his head. "No. Her health is fine. She was just the unfortunate messenger."

It's him. It isn't, Hailey argued with herself. She worked to ignore the nagging feeling in her gut and the way all the facts pointed to Gage having some sort of medical condition. He'd just said the trouble started with a conversation with his mom. Maybe he wasn't really sick. Maybe this whole misunderstanding did have something to do with her.

"Is it just that your mom's getting older, and she's all alone? Do you need to take care of her? We can do that. We could sell the house, move closer. I could find another job." Hailey hated how desperate she sounded, but this might be her only shot to convince Gage that they could work through whatever the problem was. "Or, your mom could come live with us. We don't have to have a nursery. We could put the crib in our room, or we don't even have to have a baby right away." Her mind switched gears fast, producing solution after solution, adjustments to their perfect plans, almost quicker than her tongue could get them out.

Gage gave a weary sigh, squeezed her fingers lightly, then withdrew his hand and leaned back in his chair. "Nothing is wrong with my mom. No stroke. No memory or other age-related issues. She doesn't even have a cold. She's happy where she lives. She has a bunch of girlfriends—other widows like herself—and they have a good time together."

"Oh." Hailey stiffened in her own chair. Amura began fussing, no doubt frustrated with the lack of attention. Hailey shifted position again, cradled Amura's head in the crook of her arm, and began rocking side to side.

"It means a lot that you'd give up all that for my mom—for me."

"For *us*, Gage. I'd give those things up to be with you. A house is just a house. A business is just a business."

"Still," he said. "I know how much both mean to you. You've worked so hard for each. You're a planner and a dreamer, Hailey. I've never met someone more so. It's one of the things I love most about you."

Love. Present tense. As in, he still did?

"But..." There was still a *but* somewhere. *Something* had changed his mind. "Did I plan too much for our wedding?" With her female entourage made up of her mother and sisters, she could see that was entirely possible. At one point Gage *had* said he'd hoped for something more simple.

"This isn't about the wedding or any of your plans. But your dreams—"

He broke off and looked up at the ceiling, lips pressed together and brow furrowed in frustration. She gave him his moment, biting her tongue, forcing herself to listen instead of continuing attempts to guess the problem or pry it from him. The seconds passed, lengthening into what had to be a minute or more.

"You'll make a great mother someday." Gage nodded toward Amura, and Hailey looked down to see that the baby had fallen asleep in her arms. Hailey's gaze lifted to Gage's face. The longing etched in his expression gave her hope.

"I should probably be married first." It was becoming painful to swallow, to breathe.

"Yeah." He wouldn't look at her again, but kept his eyes on Amura. "No doubt you will be. Any man would be lucky to have you."

"Except—you?" Her voice faltered again. *He's slipping away.*

"Including me." Gage's mouth set in a stoic line. "But I can't. I can't be the husband you need or give you the life you deserve. I wish I could, Hailey. I wish it more than anything, but this is out of my control. I'm so sorry I hurt you. When I broke our engagement it was to spare you hurt."

To spare me! Hailey wanted to shout at him but instead felt tears slipping down her cheeks. "Nothing is unfixable."

"This is." His mouth turned down as his own eyes misted. "I can't give you the life we planned, so I'm setting you free to find it with someone else. Because I love you that much." Gage stood quickly, leaned forward, and pressed a kiss to her forehead. "Be happy," he whispered. "For both of us."

16

Once in a Lifetime

GAGE HELD THE door for Meghan, then followed her inside the crowded mall. *This should be fun.* He opened the envelope and withdrew the list Lucy had given him with the cash for Christmas shopping. "Size 6X. What does that mean?" He held out the paper listing Aimee's clothing needs, as proof that he hadn't made the size up. "Is it a typo?"

"Nope. Follow me, clueless." Meghan flashed him a grin that bordered on evil and began her march down the mall, heading toward some store, unknown to him, that she'd insisted would have every item of clothing they needed. Gage limped along beside her, weaving in and out of the Honolulu Christmas shopper traffic, each step on his sore leg a painful reminder of last night and the ache in his heart that only seemed to be getting worse.

After talking with Hailey he'd hoped to feel better, that a softer breakup would somehow lessen the hurt of losing her. But if anything, the opposite was true.

It's really, truly over. You couldn't break a woman's heart twice and expect otherwise. And he didn't. It had never been his intention to get back together with Hailey. He'd considered briefly, yesterday, that they might remain friends, but he'd realized last night how difficult, if not impossible, that would be. He didn't want to be around to see her fall in love with another guy. He hoped she did eventually, because he truly wished her every happiness. He just wasn't man enough to stay around to watch it. Being near Hailey in the coming weeks and months would be just like Nurse Nice from the hospital last night, gleefully pouring antiseptic on his wound and watching him writhe in agony. No thanks.

"Hurry up, Gimp Along," Meghan called. She folded her arms and stood, toe tapping, as she waited for him to catch up.

He was surprised she waited at all and that she hadn't outright kicked him in his injured shin when he'd given her the brief explanation of what had caused his injury. Meghan seemed to have developed a protective streak where Hailey was concerned, and Gage's admission of his mess up last night certainly hadn't swayed things in his favor. But instead of telling him what an idiot he was, she'd listened quietly, her brow creased in apparent deep thought.

She hadn't said another word about it, until now.

"Explain the sizing, please," he urged Meghan once he caught up. He felt grateful that she'd agreed to help him, though she'd been assigned to shop for another child. She'd taken pity on Gage—or perhaps on Aimee, fearing what he would buy for her if left on his own.

"Think of it as a half size," Meghan said. "6X is larger than a six, but not as large as a size seven."

"So all girls' clothing sizes are like that? 4X, 5X, 6X? That seems a little messed up." Gage tucked the paper back in his pocket as they walked. "I mean, no wonder women are self-conscious about what size they wear. An X in men's clothing means extra large. So basically from childhood on up, girls who wear an X size are labeled as extra large."

Meghan laughed. "It's not like that. 6X is the *only* X size. There aren't any others."

"Even weirder." Gage rolled his eyes.

"Not really." She stopped in front of a large store front featuring only children's clothing. "I used to work here—in Arizona, of course. The sizing has to do with little girls' growth patterns. A lot of six-year-old girls have growth spurts, necessitating an in-between size."

"Ah." Gage nodded. "Guess that makes sense—sort of. What other secrets did you learn that you can pass on to me—before I step across the threshold into this unknown world?" He leaned forward, peered inside, and had his suspicions confirmed. Not a single male in the store.

Might as well be going into JoAnn's. Though he'd have felt slightly more comfortable there. After they'd purchased the house, and when they were remodeling the downstairs, he'd gone with Hailey to look at fabric samples for curtains and upholstery a time or two.

Meghan folded her arms across her middle. "Sparkles."

"Huh?"

"Little girls like sparkles—you know, bling. Sequins and shiny fabric. They also like ponies and unicorns and rainbows. With Aimee, I don't think you can go wrong with pink. And if you can find something really soft and furry, or if you can find some leggings with a tutu attached, that would probably be a really big hit with her. Just think about the way she was twirling every time she got excited when we were building the playhouse."

Leggings? What the heck were those? Maybe she meant those sweater-sleeve things that women sometimes wore on their lower legs to keep warm. He'd never seen Hailey with a pair, but then she'd never really followed the latest fashion trends.

"Okay. Got it," Gage lied. "Furry horses, sparkly stuff, and a pink muumuu." Just the thought of fur and a muumuu elevated his heartbeat. He couldn't forget last night fast enough.

"Come on." Meghan grabbed his hand and pulled him into the store. She handed him a shopping bag and gave him a push over to the left. "That side of the store is girls. Stay over there, and at least you'll have a prayer of getting this right."

"You won't go far?" Gage asked.

"I'll be right here too," she assured him. "I promise not to leave until you're done. That way if everything you pick out is hideous, I can let you know."

"I'm sure you will." Gage stood still a moment, taking in the sea of pink fleece surrounding him. Meghan had deposited him right in the middle of the pajama section. He pulled a pair that looked like they might fit Aimee off the rack and checked the size. *10. Maybe not.* He put it back quickly. His mom was so going to hear about this. This trip kept going from bad to worse. The shock of seeing Hailey and reopening that wound, last night's epic disaster, ensuing injury and near jail time, and now being completely out of his league shopping for a little girl. This had to be a once-in-a-lifetime event. *I'll never do this again.*

The thought stopped him. He wouldn't do this again. Ever. The nieces and nephews he'd counted as his were really Hailey's. And now that he wasn't getting married and having children of his own, he really never would shop for a child at Christmas again. The thought plowed into him as hard as the dog had last night.

Never again. Loss washed over him, especially as he thought of Hailey holding that baby this afternoon. Everything he really wanted had been encapsulated in that one moment.

Loss. Micah had talked to everyone about that principle last night, about how they were all here because they'd lost something and were powerless to get it back. Even Ray, on top of the world with his new life now, couldn't reclaim those years he'd wasted. He couldn't go back and change his actions to not hurt those who'd been negatively affected by them—like his friend who'd died from an overdose. He would never be able to say to a future employer that he hadn't done time for drugs. But Ray had learned that he could use his loss to help others, and he could find joy in it, in life.

Now that Gage had said what he'd wanted to Hailey, he hoped he could move on. The key to that, he knew, was finding happiness in other experiences life had to offer. He had to cut his losses, so to speak, and enjoy what life could still give him.

Even and including this experience shopping for Aimee.

Enjoy. This. He began sliding the hangers on the rack one at a time, looking at each pair of pajamas, noting how soft the fabric was and looking at the print before he even checked the size. If he came to a pair he liked, he paused and thought of Aimee and tried to decide if she would like them too. When he'd gone through almost the entire rack, he found a nightgown with flowers on it that looked just like the ones Aimee had filled the playhouse boxes with yesterday.

Perfect. He remembered the way she'd shoved the plastic petals to her nose and proclaimed them pretty.

Gage selected a 6X and checked the paper to see what else Aimee needed. *Underwear.* Just his luck. He found some with ponies and rainbows on them in bins near the register. This was easier than he'd imagined.

Three dresses came next, each with a full skirt for twirling. Meghan was right. Aimee really was a twirler. Yesterday he'd wondered how she could go around so many times without getting dizzy and falling down. He bought a pink sweater and a yellow sweater to go over the dresses on cool mornings, then on impulse added a pair of sparkly purple rain boots and a raincoat and umbrella to match, even though those weren't on the list. Any little girl who liked to twirl also probably liked to dance in the rain.

Meghan finished before he did and seemed genuinely impressed when she found him again, nodding her approval and telling him how cute everything he'd selected was. By then Gage had added hair bows and bands, slippers with bunny heads, red sparkly shoes, and four sets of shorts and T-shirts that could be mixed and matched. He wondered which outfit Aimee would choose to wear first and felt something akin to genuine happiness when he thought about her opening her gifts Christmas morning.

"She needs a doll," he said to Meghan as they wove their way through the baby section on their way to the register.

"The toy store is next," Meghan told him. "Maybe I'll have you pick out the toys for my little guy, too, since you've done such a great job here."

"I've been around a lot of kids." He realized how true that was, at least for the last year and a half. Any activity with Hailey's family meant children. Lots of them. He hadn't realized how much he'd picked up from those experiences. He hadn't realized how much he enjoyed them.

How much I'm going to miss them.

The image of Hailey holding the baby this afternoon flashed in his mind again as he passed a display of cream-colored knit baby dresses, booties, and hats. Gage paused, surprised to see outfits like that, meant for babies in obviously cooler climates, for sale here in Hawaii.

Again he thought of the baby Hailey had been holding. Micah had told him the child's mother had died and that the little girl wouldn't be here long. The orphanage wasn't set up for babies. In the coming weeks she would be adopted, either by a family here in Hawaii, or possibly one on the mainland.

"That's definitely not a 6X, and, no, they don't sell doll clothes here." Meghan inclined her head toward the registers. "Ready?"

"Almost." Gage picked up the little dress and placed it in his bag, then grabbed a pair of the booties and one of the hats. "This is for someone else," he said casually. Maybe, if the baby ended up going to the mainland, she could wear it the day she met her new family.

An hour later they left the toy store, Gage loaded down with bags containing everything from a doll that talked, to a tea set, play dough, Candyland, Chutes and Ladders, and Cootie, a bucket of Legos, and a dozen books. "The kids at the orphanage have stockings, right?" he asked as they passed a See's Candy store. "Maybe we should get some candy and treats to go in them."

"You are really into this." Meghan paused, hands on her hips as she looked at him. "I'm not sure what's changed with you this afternoon, but I have to say, I like it."

"Nothing's changed," Gage said. "Not really."

"You and Hailey didn't patch things up?" Meghan asked hopefully, then answered her own question before he could. "Guess not. If that were the case she'd be shopping with you instead."

"We talked," Gage said. "It's still over, but I feel better about how it ended. I hope she knows I wasn't just being a jerk."

Meghan's shoulders sagged. "Never said you were a jerk. Just stupid. Both of you, apparently."

"Call me whatever you'd like." Gage sidestepped her and headed for the candy store. "But leave Hailey out of it. She's creative and intelligent and has the smartest brain for business I've ever known."

"All that may be true," Meghan said. "But if she's really that bright, she'd be smart enough to figure out how to get you back."

17

Retail Therapy

"Nothing beats retail therapy and fresh chocolate chip cookies." Kirsten held out The Cookie Company box. "You have to try one of these. They're still warm."

"Thanks." Hailey tucked the bulging Macy's bag under her arm and reached for a cookie. She took a bite, then closed her eyes, enjoying a moment of bliss. "Almost as good as Mom—homemade," Hailey amended, glancing quickly at Kirsten.

"Actually, these are better than my mom's," Kirsten said. "She wasn't much of a cook. We ate out a lot."

"I'm sorry," Hailey said, silently berating herself, yet again, for saying the wrong thing. "Not that you ate out a lot, but for saying something in the first place, for the reminder—of your mom."

Kirsten shook her head. "Don't be. Just about everything is a reminder. Mothers and daughters are a pretty common phenomenon, you know?" She attempted a smile. "Ever since she died, I feel like people have tried to avoid bringing it up, and they avoid me because they're afraid of accidentally saying something."

"And that's worse, because then you're even more alone—lonely." *Been there, done that the past month.* Hailey imagined it must be a million times worse for Kirsten. Friends avoiding you was one thing, but not having a mom to complain to about it... "Tell me about your mother," Hailey said. "If you want to, that is."

"After this bite," Kirsten mumbled, wiping crumbs from her mouth. "Those really are delicious. We should buy more before we leave."

"Good idea." Hailey wasn't sure how she'd hold one more bite. They'd sampled everything, from the soft pretzel offerings to Orange Julius to some amazing fried rice—the occasion demanded comfort food. And shopping. Her arms were full of bags filled with clothing, stuffed animals, and books for Amura, dresses for Hailey's sisters, shell necklaces for her nieces, gummy leis for her nephews, a game for Charlie—in case Brock's choice of presents turned out not to be great—a new ring for Allyson, and other assorted gifts for family members and her new friends. She couldn't remember the last time she'd spent so much money or enjoyed it, or *needed* retail therapy, quite so much. An over-indulgence in both food and spending seemed just what the doctor ordered, and completely justified, after her conversation with Gage.

Fortunately the Windward Mall in Kaneohe had the stores, shoppers, Christmas decorations and music to work effectively as a Band-Aid until later, when Hailey knew she'd rehash every word of their conversation and fall apart again.

On the ride over she'd asked Kirsten if she'd like company while shopping. Allyson seemed to have taken Lisbeth under her wing, and Meghan had gone in the van with those going to Honolulu. Hailey hadn't really cared where she shopped. Some things for her family she planned to order online anyway. But feeling every bit as awful as she had the day after Thanksgiving, when Gage had broken up with her the first time, Hailey had doubted the outing would be much fun. *Unless...*

Taking a lesson from both her mother and Lucy, she'd looked outside of herself until she'd found the person she thought most likely needed a friend today. At brunch she'd learned that it was Kirsten who had lost her mom. She was probably used to shopping with her, and Hailey guessed this might be a hard day. Hailey knew she was a poor substitute, but she'd invited Kirsten to shop with her anyway, and Kirsten had eagerly accepted.

Three hours later, Hailey could say she'd genuinely had a good time. Looking outside herself was more than good advice; it might just be what got her through the rest of this trip. This morning's magic with the turtles, and Gage there with her, felt like it had happened weeks ago. This afternoon his words had rung with such finality, and sincerity, that they'd squelched what hope she'd had for something changing between them.

It's over. As over as Kirsten's time with her mom.

Forcing her thoughts from Gage, Hailey focused all her attention on listening to Kirsten as they walked the length of the mall a second time. Once started on the subject of her mom, Kirsten didn't need prompting to keep going. She told Hailey all about growing up in a household with just the two of them. Friday-night pizza and sleepovers in Mom's bed, monthly summer trips to the drive-in theater, the city, and the beach, the Christmas tradition of hiding presents from each other in the most unusual places, then leaving them there Christmas morning, so that there was always a treasure hunt involved.

"I think Mom did that so the morning would last longer. She always worried about me because I didn't have any siblings. She knew other families ate lavish breakfasts and opened presents for hours because there were more people involved. So she made sure to have grocery-store cinnamon rolls and a way to make opening our presents last longer." Kirsten paused in front of the Hallmark store. "One of those was always a new ornament for our tree—something to remember the year by."

"Where are all those ornaments now?" Hailey asked.

"In storage." Kirsten pulled her gaze from the festive display in the window. "I didn't unpack any of the Christmas things this year. I just couldn't."

Hailey thought of her plain apartment above the shop. Before Thanksgiving she'd had big plans for decorating, starting with the tree she and Gage were supposed to cut down. Since there had been no Gage, there had been no tree, and she hadn't seen the point in decorating for a holiday she was no longer looking forward to.

"Next year," Hailey said, as much to herself as to Kirsten. "Your mom would want you to celebrate. She'd be sad to think you missed it." *Be happy,* Gage had said. *For both of us.* Would he even be around to see Christmas next year? Her eyes stung suddenly.

"I need to get some wrapping paper for all of these." She held up her bags a second, then hurried into the store before Kirsten could notice her tears. Hailey grabbed a couple of rolls of wrapping paper, then, after checking to see that Kirsten was busy reading greeting cards, headed straight to the ornaments. There weren't a lot of choices left this close to Christmas, but she found one with shells that said, "The beach is calling."

"Perfect." Hailey brought it to the register, grabbing a pack of festive note cards on the way, then paid for both along with the wrapping paper.

"Ready?" she asked Kirsten, who was still looking at cards. "It's almost time for the van to come back for us."

"After we get more cookies?" Kirsten juggled her own packages as they headed that direction.

"Sure." Hailey's stomach protested at the thought of another bite—of anything right now.

"Thank you for this." Kirsten stopped suddenly, in the middle of the crowded mall, and turned to face Hailey. "I really needed someone today. So far this week's been pretty good, but shopping was one of those things Mom and I used to do. And I was dreading it." She leaned forward, throwing an arm around Hailey in an impulsive hug. "I just miss her so much."

Hailey dropped all her packages, letting the heavy ones slide to the floor as gently as possible, so she could return Kirsten's hug. Channeling her own mom's comforting ability, she held on tight. "You're going to be okay. It's just going to take some time."

Kirsten's words rang through Hailey's mind and changed to her own. *I just miss Gage so much.* That was the common thread they all shared this week. Allyson missed her husband and her best friend; Kirsten missed her mom. Meghan missed her parents as they used to be. Caleb missed his wife and baby. Lisbeth and Brock missed their health. *And I miss Gage so much it literally feels like there is a hole in my heart.*

What was it going to take for any of them to truly recover? Could they?

A woman bumped Hailey as she passed, and Kirsten leaned back, an embarrassed smile accompanying her tear-filled eyes. "Sorry. I didn't plan that very well."

"Like we ever get to choose the timing." Hailey reached down to pick up their packages. "Don't let it bother you. If people can't be compassionate and understanding two days before Christmas . . . This world is hopeless."

She didn't want it to be and didn't want to feel that way herself. *Do something for someone else.*

"Let's go get those cookies—enough to bring back to share."

"Good idea." Kirsten turned away, and they began walking once more.

The thought of even one cookie or food of any kind still made Hailey ill, but she hoped Micah wouldn't mind stopping at a grocery store later today or tomorrow. She needed to pick up some cinnamon rolls for Christmas morning.

18

O, Christmas Tree

"Dinner was perfect, ladies. Thank you for cooking tonight." Lucy swept through the kitchen on her way to who-knew-what other errand. The woman was always on the move.

"You're welcome," they chorused.

"Come back later for dessert," Allyson called, leaning over to inspect the pies baking in the oven. "Who knew Hawaii could smell like this?" She smiled dreamily as the mingled scents of apple and pumpkin filled the kitchen.

The grand piano in the other room came suddenly to life with an explosion of chords that Hailey soon recognized as a sophisticated arrangement of "Joy to the World." She continued drying the platters Meghan had hand-washed, while Lisbeth loaded the dishwasher and Kirsten put together the leftovers to be taken to the homeless—a routine, Hailey had learned, that was followed after every meal here. Lucy and Micah seemed aware of every need on this island and beyond.

"I've been wanting to talk to you," Meghan said, as she handed Hailey a bowl to dry. "Last night I was out of line. I'm really sorry."

"It's all right—understandable." Through deduction Hailey had realized that Meghan's parents were the ones going through the bitter divorce. "Gage and I talked today. I'll be all right." *Not really.* Actually, she felt worse. Had her relationship with Gage been such that he felt she'd just up and leave when something bad happened? That he hadn't even attempted to trust her with his problem but had decided she'd be better off without him hurt deeply and had her questioning everything about their relationship from day one.

"I know he still loves you," Meghan said.

Hailey nodded. "He told me as much."

"So?" Meghan bounced excitedly on her toes. "It's obvious you feel the same."

"He's trying to protect me from something," Hailey said. "He doesn't want me involved." She moved past Meghan, heading for the island where the serving dishes were kept. She didn't really want to talk about this anymore. What she needed was to think about it a whole lot more, to make sense of it and then figure out how to proceed from here. Between shopping and making dinner, what little time she'd had in private to think over the conversation with Gage today, she had finally made the jump from sad to angry. And when she was angry, she generally did something about it. Her temper matched her hair, her mom said. *So be it.*

There was no way this was over—no way *she and Gage* were over. In her book love did conquer all, even if that meant adjusting her dreams or the time they had together. But he was not simply going to walk away.

Beyond that resolution, she hadn't had time to figure out how to proceed. The evening had been spent cooking and serving and eating and cleaning up. Hailey was looking forward to a hot shower and some alone time to dissect exactly what Gage had said today and how to get him to talk to her again. *To trust me.*

The carol from the piano changed to "Jingle Bells." Micah poked his head in the kitchen.

"Your presence is requested in the great room, ladies. We have a tree to decorate. And if left to the men..." He shrugged helplessly.

"Say no more." Lisbeth closed the dishwasher. "Come on, girls. It's time to save Christmas."

Hailey trooped after her along with the others, wondering just how much longer she could physically stay awake and on her feet before she collapsed. Couldn't the tree wait until tomorrow? Not to mention that her emotions were fried. Being in the same room with Gage was sheer torture. She had to be careful where she looked. She was terrified to make eye contact, afraid that if she did, she'd spontaneously combust in an explosion of tears or a burst of angry words. *How dare he not confide in me and trust that I'll stand by him! If the tables were turned...*

But when they entered the great room and saw the tree—one of the largest and prettiest she'd ever seen, in a house, at least—Hailey's exhaustion faded, replaced by something else. Longing, perhaps, for home and the holiday she'd been hoping to avoid altogether by coming here. The tallest point of the tree nearly reached the exposed beam that ran along the middle of the ceiling. The branches were full, with hundreds of lights twinkling and reflected in the wall of windows behind. Hailey felt her anger softening. Suddenly she was ten years old again, and her father had just set up the tree her family had spent the day trudging through the woods to find.

"Where'd you find *that* on an island?" Meghan asked, her mouth slightly agape as she, along with the others, craned their necks, staring up at the wonder.

"Costco," Micah said. "It's not real, but more environmentally friendly." His smile was nearly as broad as it had been this morning when discussing turtles. "The guys have assembled it, but they need some help with the rest. Feel free to boss them around. You'll find all the ornaments over there." He inclined his head toward a half dozen plastic bins stacked near the doorway.

"Let's do this." Kirsten put on a brave face. "Decorating the tree was my mom's favorite part of the holiday."

Hailey could see she was struggling and stepped forward to put an arm around her, but Allyson beat her to it.

"Then your mom would be really happy to know you're here, decorating this gorgeous tree."

Kirsten nodded and swiped at her eyes. "Yeah. She would."

"Let's make this the most beautiful tree—for her," Hailey said.

The next hour passed in a blur of red and silver and white and gold as box after box of gorgeous ornaments was unpacked. Ray and Gage stood on ladders on either side, placing the ornaments handed to them on the tallest branches. Hailey took care to avoid going to Gage's side and for the most part kept herself busy unpacking the boxes and handing ornaments to the others.

The lights were set on a mode to change from white to colors every few minutes, and Hailey found a box of decadent ribbon that she and Allyson wound carefully around the tree, in and out of the branches and around the many ornaments that had been hung. Only Darren and Lucy didn't participate. Lucy was mysteriously absent, and Darren hadn't left the baby grand, providing them a musical feast equal to the stunning tree.

After Kirsten climbed the ladder and placed the star on the very top, the lights were dimmed, and they all stood back to admire their work.

Darren's tenor voice, along with the piano, filled the space behind them with a familiar melody, though slightly altered lyrics. "The sun is shining, the sea is blue, The coconut and palm trees sway."

Allyson and Kirsten caught on and joined in. "There's never been such a day—"

"Wait," Darren shouted, waving his hand in the air for them to stop. "In beautiful La-i-e."

"That's bad." Micah shook his head but laughed softly.

"Cut me some slack," Darren grumbled good-naturedly. "I'm making this up as I go."

Hailey joined the others crowding around the piano.

"It's December the 23rd, and I—flew here in a big bird."

"Awful!" Micah shouted, but the women all clapped.

Darren ignored everyone, his focus on his hands, moving down the piano in an intricate pattern of chords leading into the chorus for "White Christmas." He waved his hand again, this time encouraging them to join in.

Hailey put her arm around Kirsten as they all sang wistfully about the Christmases they used to know. Likely every one of them wished they could go back in time to reclaim what had been lost—health, a parent, family, love.

Darren carried them all with his strong voice. Caleb sang well, too, but Hailey noticed he faltered when it came to the line about children. No doubt he was missing his little girl and wishing. *Wishing, like the rest of us, that things could somehow be different.*

"I'm dreaming..." Still thinking of home, Hailey glanced toward the tree and found Gage instead, staring at her from the other side of the piano. There was a tenderness in his gaze she recognized from the more poignant moments of their relationship. The last being the night before Thanksgiving at her parents' house, after all the others had gone to bed.

Only Hailey and Gage and her sister's newborn had still

been awake. Hailey had offered to watch the baby so her sister could get some much-needed sleep.

"You have a way with those, you know." Gage had looked down at little Sierra, awake, but content in Hailey's arms.

Hailey shrugged. "It's because I've been around them my whole life. I suppose it comes with the territory of being the youngest and having a crazy big family."

Gage had nuzzled her shoulder. "You look good with a baby. I can't wait until you're holding one of our own."

Hailey laughed. "You're going to have to wait—about eleven months, at least. And that's if everything works perfectly the first time." They'd decided months ago that if they were going to have those three or four kids they both wanted, there was no point in waiting to start a family after they married.

"It will be a tragedy if it doesn't." Gage touched her cheek. "Practicing will be torture." He'd kissed her then, a long, slow, temptingly delicious kiss that lasted until Sierra gave a cry of protest at being both ignored and partially squished between them.

Hailey remembered all of this now, and she would have sworn Gage was thinking about it, too, before he looked away. Tears burned at the back of her eyes and spilled over, and then Meghan's arm was around her.

"We are going to *fix* this," she whispered fiercely. "We are going to find out what is wrong with that man—*your* man—and we are going to make it better."

Hailey nodded numbly, wanting to feel hope but unable to.

This isn't fixable, Gage had said. She dashed at her tears and mouthed the words to the rest of the song.

Outside the clear skies had turned cloudy, and it was raining again. Micah left the piano and threw open the double doors on either side of the room. The fresh breeze from outside came in, and while it might not have been pine-scented or snowy, Hailey couldn't help but compare the moment to the ending scene of *White Christmas*, when the barn doors were slid open and everyone saw the miraculous snow outside. Who knew Hawaii could feel so . . . Christmasy? Was there any possibility of her own miracle?

Allyson left to check on her pies, and Ray and Brock lit a fire in the large, stone fireplace at the end of the room. They filled some old-fashioned popcorn poppers and held them over the fire, while Darren continued his sojourn at the piano. Hailey alone lingered at the piano, fearful of seeing Gage again, even from across the room.

"You play beautifully," she said, moving closer to the keyboard and Darren. "It really made everyone's night."

"Thanks." Darren's fingers swept up the keys one last time, then ended on a strong G chord and were silent.

"You don't even have any music?" Hailey stared at the empty stand. "All of that was memorized? Or can you play anything by ear?"

He shook his head, a pained expression on his face as the reverberation died away. "I can't play by ear. Those were all memorized."

"That's *really* impressive." He'd played for a good hour, carol after carol.

"It was meant to be," he said sarcastically, then apologized. "I'm sorry. You were trying to compliment me, and I was rude."

"No offense taken." Hailey wondered what she'd said wrong.

"For a long time I hated playing the piano, singing—basically everything my parents wanted me to do. But maybe there's some merit in the music side of things, at least. Tonight was nice, actually kind of fun. The best time I've ever had at Christmas. But I wasn't playing to impress anyone. Those days are over, though that *is* why I know all this music."

"I guess I'm both glad and sad to hear that. I'm glad you had fun tonight, but you didn't enjoy Christmas when you were growing up? When you were a kid?"

Darren shook his head as he gently lowered the lid over the keys. "Nope. Never decorated a tree—that was always done for us, by a professional crew who brought in expensive, breakable ornaments that weren't ever to be touched. 'Maintain a five-foot radius from the tree at all times,' my mom always said. They, my parents, had a big party each year, for show of course. We had to look like the most put-together family there was. It was catered, always some fancy, not-that-great food, and the house was filled with all the big playmakers in D.C. I wasn't allowed to come until I was twelve. And then it was only to play the piano all night."

"That's how you knew all those songs," Hailey said. He *had* played well enough to play professionally.

"I'll probably go to my grave knowing those songs." Darren ran his hand along the top of the piano. "My mother made me practice for months ahead of time each year. Mistakes were unacceptable. My performance had to be flawless, perfect the entire night through, because I was just another thing to show off—like the house and the tree."

Hailey could hardly imagine this. She'd grown up in a home with a piano, too, and the most frequent songs it had played were probably "Chopsticks" and "Heart and Soul." Though she'd had lessons, she wasn't really any good. But no one ever complained when she, or any of her siblings or their kids, messed around at the piano.

And never decorating a tree . . . A yearly party with stuffy senators instead of quirky relatives. Hailey suppressed a shudder and the sudden longing for home she felt. "Is that why you're here? To have a real Christmas, I mean?"

Darren shrugged. "Partly. But it's bigger than that. I recently left my father's law firm, which is akin to leaving the family. But truthfully, it's not much family to leave. My sister and I haven't spoken in years. My mom only calls when she needs something. And I never wanted to be an attorney."

"I'm so sorry." Once again Hailey's standard answer seemed less than adequate. "I can't imagine life without my family."

"And I can no longer imagine life *with* mine. Because it's not a life." Darren stood suddenly, as if being near the piano was a reminder he didn't want.

"What *do* you want to do?" Hailey asked. "Instead of being an attorney, I mean."

"Nothing respectable." A corner of his mouth lifted in a lopsided grin. "I want to teach high school history and coach basketball. I used to be pretty good at both. I had a scholarship to play college ball, but I turned it down because Dad wanted me to attend his alma mater."

"Teachers are extremely respectable," Hailey said. "And noble—and underpaid." Coming from the life he had, that could be an adjustment. "You don't care, do you?"

"About the money or lack thereof? Nah." Darren's grin widened as he stood. "But my parents will be appalled."

"Will be? Are you going back to school, then?" Hailey followed him toward the delightful aroma of the fresh pies Allyson had just set out on the table.

"Yep. This January. The community college. Nothing fancy, but it will get me the degree I should have gotten in the first place."

"That's really—courageous. Giving up a lucrative career and the approval of your family to pursue your dream."

He shook his head. "Courage would be giving up something that mattered. Unfortunately, my family hasn't fallen into that category for a long time." Darren picked up a piece of apple pie. "Hmm. Homemade pie. Another first." He took a bite and glanced Allyson's direction. "Foolish man, that husband of hers. Giving up a woman who is not only a lovely person inside and out, but who can bake like this as well. Excuse me while I go compliment the cook."

Just so long as you don't kiss her. Allyson wasn't ready for anything like that yet and probably wouldn't be for a long time. Nor was Hailey—*with anyone but Gage.*

She chose a piece of pumpkin pie and carefully turned to face the rest of the room, her breath held tensely for the second she'd see him again.

Brock and Lisbeth were busy attempting to throw popcorn into each other's mouths, missing far more pieces than they were catching, and laughing together.

Perfect. They were good for each other. Good pen pals in the coming months, when neither would have as much to laugh about.

Kirsten was curled up on the sofa, reading a children's Christmas book.

Caleb and Ray were playing chess.

Gage was nowhere to be found. Neither was Meghan. *Uh oh.*

Hailey didn't know whether she was more relieved or worried. If Gage was sick, did his absence mean he wasn't feeling well? Or, had he decided to turn in early because she was here? Had Meghan cornered him somewhere and demanded an explanation?

Exactly what I should do. Though maybe not the demand part. They'd never had that kind of relationship, and Hailey didn't want to start now. It seemed as if she shouldn't have to ask what life-altering thing was wrong. Once, not long ago, she'd felt they could tell each other anything. No subject was taboo, no conversation off limits, no truth too frightening to trust each other with.

So why was she so afraid?

Courage. If Brock could deal with muscular dystrophy, Lisbeth could face a brain tumor, and Allyson could endure her husband's betrayal, it seemed that asking a question shouldn't be that hard.

19

Small Comfort

"GAGE, COULD YOU help me a minute?" Lucy waved to him from the, large, circular driveway in front of the resort.

"Sure." Gage changed directions. He'd been heading to his room—no more night walks for him on the beach, the bluff, or anywhere.

Lucy opened the rear door of a jeep parked beneath the overhang near the front double doors. It had the Hawaiian Holidays logo on the side, as well as the logos for Hawaiian Hope Orphanage and a couple of other business names he wasn't familiar with but that he was sure Micah and Lucy were associated with.

"Can you watch Amura for a minute while I run these things inside?" She pulled a portacrib and a duffle from the back.

"Sure," Gage said. "Or I can carry them inside for you."

"As banged up as you are, and with a leg full of stitches? I don't think so. But thanks for the offer." Lucy hefted the duffle in one hand and the portacrib in the other and headed toward the house. "Be right back."

Gage peeked through the open passenger window and saw a car seat in back. He opened the door and looked down at the baby Hailey had been reading to and then rocked to sleep this afternoon.

She was awake now, and she turned to him, her large brown eyes taking him in as a smile grew on her face.

"Hello, little one." Gage leaned in closer. She lifted her hands and waved them.

Reflex? Or does she want me to pick her up? Gage couldn't remember at what age babies did what. *Hailey would know.* He brought a hand to his head, though the pain wasn't there. He felt his loss everywhere. The pull of the stitches biting into his skin as he walked was nothing compared to what he'd felt just a little while ago, watching Hailey standing there at the piano, singing.

The scene had been all too reminiscent of times he'd had with her at her parents' house. And it was all too similar to the scenes he'd imagined for their own lives in the coming years. The magnitude of his loss had hit him again, as fresh as if it was the day after Thanksgiving, his own personal *Black Friday,* all over again.

Amura began to fuss, her arms still outstretched. Gage didn't know if he was supposed to get her out of her car seat or not, but the desire he had to hold her overrode any thought of whether he ought to try to keep her happy another way or wait until Lucy returned.

If Christmas shopping for a child this afternoon had been a once-in-a-lifetime experience, he had to imagine that holding a baby wouldn't be an opportunity he had too often either.

He reached down, unbuckling the seat straps with ease, thanks to lots of practice with Hailey's nieces and nephews.

How many single men can do that? He felt the tiniest bit smug as he lifted the baby, brought her to his shoulder, and began bouncing. She was soft and warm and had that baby smell Hailey always talked about.

"What if our babies smell different?" he'd asked her one

night when she was *oohing* and *ahhing* and sighing happily as she held Sierra, her face nestled in the peach fuzz atop the baby's head.

"Impossible," Hailey had said. "All babies smell this way. It's so their parents fall in love with them at once."

Gage didn't know about that, but Amura had that same, pleasant aroma just now, and as they swayed together in the dark under the overhang, with the rain pitter-pattering softly on the roof, he felt himself falling a little in love.

Dangerous business. It had been one thing to find joy in shopping for a child; it would be quite another to become attached to one that wasn't his.

He didn't need any more hurt or heartache. He'd reached his fill already and had been heading to his room to make arrangements to get out of here. While he was grateful he'd had the opportunity for better closure with Hailey, nothing good could come from being here longer.

Every day was another day closer to when they were to have been married. Instead of getting easier, it was only getting worse—for both of them. He hadn't missed the tears glistening in her eyes tonight. It had taken every shred of willpower he had to walk out of that room, instead of sweeping her in his arms, begging her forgiveness, and kissing away her sorrow.

It was his fault she was crying in the first place, and the only way to start to make things better was to get out of her life completely. As soon as possible. Before Christmas.

Given his intentions to leave, maybe holding a baby and feeling a little comfort for a few minutes wasn't such a terrible thing after all.

"Aren't you two a team?" Lucy breezed past him and closed the back door of the jeep.

"You're welcome to keep holding Amura for a while. She

won't need to eat for some time yet, and then you can feed her, too, if you'd like."

It was a tempting offer. There was something about a baby—or this one, at least—that soothed him.

"I've got a couple of phone calls to make." Reluctantly he handed Amura to Lucy.

She looked at him askance as she gathered Amura close and grabbed a baby blanket from the jeep.

"Goodnight," Gage said and started across the wet lawn.

"You're going the wrong way, Gage. I know. I've gone that way myself before."

"What do you mean?" He could see his bungalow from here. A straight walk across the lawn, or a curved walk along the cement path. How many ways could there be to get there?

She stepped closer to him, still bundling Amura. Lucy's face held a tightness that Gage had never noticed before. "You think that because you can't have life the way you wanted it, you can't have love. It doesn't work that way. Just because your life isn't the neat box you planned, doesn't mean there isn't another box with your name on it, or another plan."

For a moment he'd forgotten that Lucy knew all about him—and Hailey. Gage shoved his hands in his pockets and looked past Lucy. "They weren't just my plans. They were Hailey's—her dreams as well as mine. Just because they've been stolen from me, doesn't mean I have to make her suffer the same."

"Ah." Lucy gave him a sad smile. "Have you considered that she's suffering an even worse loss?" Lucy shifted Amura to her other side. "You had a choice to keep some of your dream. She didn't. You took the whole thing away from her, without even trusting that she might want to keep what she could, and that she might be very willing to open up another box, to try another dream with you and be every bit as happy as she was with the first."

"You don't know Hailey like I do," Gage said. "She has this big family, and she loves kids. She's great with babies—"

"So are you." Lucy looked down at Amura. "There's more than one way to be a parent, Gage. And many more ways to have children in your life and love them. Just open your eyes—and your heart—before it's too late, and you'll see."

20

Half a Man

LEAVING THE OTHERS to continue to enjoy the evening's festivities, Hailey headed for the door, intending to slip outside and find Gage's room, and was met by Lucy coming in, a squirming, crying bundle in her arms.

She pulled back the blanket partially covering the bundle, revealing a familiar head of dark curls. "Amura didn't like being covered up, but I didn't want her to get rained on."

The entire room seemed to have frozen, its occupants fixated on the crying baby in Lucy's arms. Micah, alone, seemed capable of movement. He started toward Lucy, an unspoken question, and what almost seemed a hopeful vulnerability, clearly visible in his puzzled expression.

Tracking his progress across the floor, Hailey watched the unspoken exchange, wondering if she was the only one noticing.

As Micah drew closer Lucy met his questioning gaze and gave a sad smile and a slight shake of her head. "The orphanage isn't equipped for this—for babies, especially one who had recent surgery. I decided we'd better keep her here until we can get her on the way to her new parents."

Micah gave a little nod and put on his signature smile, not quite entirely hiding his disappointment. "So what's the plan, boss?"

Lucy glanced around the room. "Shifts? We all pitch in to take care of Amura? What do you say?"

"Of course." Hailey spoke before she'd really had a chance to think about it. But was it even a question, really? An adorable baby needed care for a couple of days, and there were twelve adults here. Plus, it was Christmas. How did one even celebrate Christmas without a baby around to love? After all, it was the birth of a baby that had started it all.

"I'll take the first shift, if you'd like." Telling herself that her motives were altruistic and not simply a means to avoid the situation with Gage, Hailey crossed the room, arms stretched out.

"I'll help out next," Caleb said. "I've had a little experience." He shrugged. "Should have been more."

Lucy gave a relieved sigh. "Thank you, both."

"Sign me up next," Micah said. "I'm always good for a late-night or early-morning snuggle."

Hailey took Amura from Lucy, who pulled out her clipboard and began writing down who would babysit and when.

"Look at the pretty tree." Hailey bounced Amura lightly as she went to stand beside it. Amura's eyes grew large as she stared at the lights and slurped happily on her fist. Hailey held her close and took comfort from Amura's sweet baby smell.

By this time next year . . . She and Gage had talked about how fun it would be to have a newborn next Christmas. She still didn't know what had changed his mind overnight about everything. *How could he expect me to accept that and move on?*

Allyson finished serving pie and joined them. Hailey went to sit beside her on the couch.

"She's adorable." Allyson smiled at Amura and received a drooly, two-teeth grin in return. "Brian and I wanted to have children, but the timing never seemed right. Now I'm not sure if I'm grateful for that or not. I wouldn't want my child to have to deal with this, but if I had one, I wouldn't be all alone."

"You're not alone, remember?" Hailey set Amura in Allyson's lap. "Not this week and not when you get home. You're coming to see me next month, and then I'm going to visit you. And in between we're going to call each other—frequently."

"I know." Allyson sighed. "It's just that the house is empty with only me in it. But I don't want to give it up. I don't want *them* to have it."

"Are you sure about that?" Kirsten sat on the ottoman in front of them. "Sorry. Not trying to interfere. But if the house is just going to make you sad, why not sell it? Or, if your ex really wants it, make him buy you out, then use that money to start on new dreams."

"I know that makes sense." Allyson paused, one hand stroking Amura's curls. "But I can't do that—yet. When the divorce is final, I'll face the reality that my marriage is really over. But until then, if there's even a chance . . ."

Hailey knew what she meant. Earlier today she'd all but convinced herself there was no chance with Gage, that after this week he would no longer be a part of her life. But she couldn't just let him go. The way he'd been looking at her tonight seemed proof of that. Just like when she'd seen him here at dinner that first night. He wasn't over her any more than she was over him. So why should she let him call it quits so easily?

"Do you mind watching Amura for a few minutes?" Hailey asked Allyson. "I need to do a couple of things before I settle in for my babysitting shift."

"Take your time." Allyson cuddled Amura. "This is the best kind of therapy."

"I know." Hailey wasn't sure what she would have done this afternoon without Amura to hold and take care of after Gage had said what he had and then left.

The men's bungalows were on the opposite side of the pool. With only five doors to knock on, Hailey figured it wouldn't be difficult to locate Gage—so long as he answered. Without bothering to stop at her room first for a jacket, and heedless of the rain, she ran across the courtyard to the other side.

The first three windows were dark, but light shone through the louvered slats of the fourth. With determined steps, Hailey strode toward the door, stopping only when she heard Gage's voice coming from inside.

"At this point I don't really care what it costs. I just need to get out of here—for Hailey's sake as well as mine. It's not good for us to be around each other if we can't be together."

Hailey stood frozen, waiting for a reply. *Who is he talking to?* No reply came, but Gage spoke again.

"I can't, Mom. And it's not that I'm worried she wouldn't understand. It wouldn't be fair of me to ask that of her. Nothing has changed since I found out. I love her too much to expect her to love half a man."

What? Hailey stepped under the eaves both to avoid the rain and to hear better.

"It's not a choice she should have to make, and I'm afraid if I stay any longer I might end up asking her to anyway."

More silence. Hailey tried to imagine his mom's response.

"If I can't find a flight I'll get a hotel in Honolulu or something, but I'd rather be with you for Christmas than on a beach alone somewhere."

Gage, leaving? Because—half a man? What did he mean? She raised her hand to knock but hesitated at the last second.

Just ask him, already. Confront him. Something stopped her, and she didn't think it was lack of courage. Or maybe it was. What if he did explain, if he clarified exactly what was wrong with him, and she reacted poorly? That would only confirm his decision that they should break up. *Better that I'm prepared.* She couldn't botch this conversation. She had one chance to get it right.

21

All is Calm

AMURA WAS AN easy baby, much less fussy than Hailey's sister's latest, Sierra. By ten-thirty Hailey had returned from her walk in the rain and the illuminating, one-sided conversation she'd heard outside of Gage's room. She'd changed Amura's diaper and dressed her in a pair of lightweight footie pajamas, pulling the zipper with extra care as it passed over the scar on the baby's chest.

Everyone else went off to bed while Hailey sterilized a bottle in the kitchen and simultaneously bounced Amura on her hip. She'd done this dozens of times, and the routine reminded her of home as perhaps nothing else could have. After feeding Amura, Hailey walked her back and forth in front of the tree until they were both almost asleep. Amura finally succumbed, and Hailey lay back on the couch, baby on top of her. Hailey found Amura's sweet scent and even breathing a comfort.

Half a man. It didn't take Hailey's thoughts long to return to Gage. Did he have to have surgery? Have something removed? Did he have something like Brock's MD? She could see that being in a wheelchair could make a guy feel like half a man. *I wouldn't see him that way.*

Or was it something even more serious and immediate? What had warranted a hospital stay last night?

The answers she sought weren't any clearer than before. There was only one thing she'd gleaned from their conversation this afternoon and the one she'd overheard Gage having with his mom. *He loves me so much he's willing to let me go.* He didn't want her to have to choose to stay or to leave.

Stubborn man. Two could play that game. She was just as stubborn, and she loved *him* so much she wasn't willing to let him go through whatever it was by himself.

And if he is sick? If it's something terminal? Her eyes stung. She blinked away the moisture, as if not crying was somehow a show of strength. *We will make the most of whatever time we have together.*

But if it's not—She'd be so grateful, so relieved.

Even if that means we can't have the family we both wanted? This thought stopped her, made her heart rate quicken suddenly. Hailey sat up, Amura still cradled close to her chest.

I can't give you the life we planned.

In her mind she saw Gage's sorrowful expression. She hadn't understood what he meant. They'd planned a lot of things for their life together, starting with—a family.

Children. What if he can't have children?

She sat unmoving for an entire minute, then two, hardly able to breathe for the pain accompanying this possibility. *None. Never.* She thought of the nursery they'd already painted, how it would be to feel the baby they'd create together stirring inside of her, the Christmases she'd imagined, finally having a child of her own at family gatherings. She'd dreamed of birthdays and trips to the beach, teaching their little ones to ride bikes and read. All of those dreams and fantasies swept through her mind and fled until it, and she, felt empty.

Plans could be altered. Houses sold, jobs changed. *But your dreams . . .* Gage had said.

I can't give you the life we planned.

We. The two of us together. If her hunch was right, he'd lost his dreams too. And worse, he had to be dealing with something more, something serious. Some kind of terrible cancer or rare illness. It was likely he wasn't just mourning the loss of the ability to have children, but a potential loss of life.

The tears that had been hovering slipped down Hailey's face. The lights on the Christmas tree blurred before her eyes, and she wondered again if Gage would be here a year from now. Six months? Or might they be blessed with five years? Still so much less than they'd planned. Why had they wasted a month already?

She drew in a ragged breath. *No children. Maybe no husband for very long either.* Could she live with that? Or would it be better to walk away now, to seal off the hurt before it could burrow any deeper? She imagined herself in a hospital, seated beside Gage, watching a monitor's blip recording his last breaths. Was that what lay in store if she stayed?

Hailey rocked back and forth, tears falling freely—so much for strength—and Amura held tight in her arms. *No family. No future that we planned. Just Gage, for whatever time he has left.*

Could she accept those terms?

I already have. The vows they'd planned to speak had included those about for better and for worse, in sickness and in health. But saying them aloud in a church didn't make them any stronger than they were already. She'd made those commitments, the promise to love Gage no matter what came their way, months earlier when she'd agreed to be his wife and he'd slipped that ring on her finger.

A subtle peace stole over her, a tranquility she hadn't expected and hadn't felt for weeks. Her tears stopped falling.

Her vision cleared, as did her mind. She glanced at her left hand and knew exactly what she needed to do. Everything was going to be all right.

As all right as it can be.

Tonight's gratitude list was even easier to come up with—maybe because everything just seemed better with a baby asleep on your stomach. Certainly because she felt hope.

Hailey held her phone in her hand and typed her list as best she could, while holding Amura. She'd forgotten the notebook in her room, but she couldn't forget to record these. Already this seemed to have become a habit she needed to keep up. To not be grateful, or not take the time to reflect on that, simply seemed wrong.

Tonight her last item had moved up to its rightful place, topping the list.

1. I'm grateful Gage is here.
2. I'm grateful for Amura.
3. I'm grateful for sea turtles and sunrises.
4. I'm grateful for Christmas trees and carols and new friends.
5. I'm grateful for love.

22

Alternate Endings

THE COUCH WAS comfortable until about three-seventeen in the morning—the time Hailey's watch showed when she awoke. For a moment she was confused about where she was and whose baby was asleep in the portacrib beside her.

As she sat up and stretched, the door from the hall leading to Lucy's and Micah's room opened. A shadowy figure crept in, something large and bulky in his hands, eerily illuminated into a monstrous shape by the lights on the Christmas tree.

"Oh good, you're awake." The shadowed figure paused, leaned forward, and set his burden down with a thud. Amura stirred in her bed.

"Micah?" Hailey rose, ready to defend the baby if need be.

"Yeah. I switched shifts with Caleb. He's not doing so well, and Lucy thought it would be better if he took his turn a little later. I'm here to take over if you want to get some better sleep."

"That would be nice." Hand at her hip, Hailey leaned back, stretching. "Between digging holes and pouring concrete, then kayaking and crisscrossing the mall, I'm feeling a bit wiped out."

"In other words, you're having a really great week." Micah came closer, his signature grin made more amusing by a serious case of bed head and a pair of dog-print, faded flannel pajama bottoms that looked like they were about twenty years old.

"It has been pretty good." Hailey reached down to pull a light blanket over Amura.

"Just pretty good, huh?" Micah scratched the scruff covering his chin. "Guess we'd better step up our game. Would you have preferred swimming with sharks to kayaking with turtles?"

Hailey held up a hand. "No! Please no. The turtles were fabulous. Everything has been. It's just some personal stuff I'm working through still."

"Ah." Micah crossed the room, pulling the thing he'd brought—an antique-looking rocker—with him. "I'm sorry about that. Lucy is too. When we selected each of you for the program, we had no idea you and Gage knew each other. I'm sure that's been awkward."

"Yes." *He knows?* She supposed Gage must have said something to him. Hailey had thought about talking to Lucy about the situation, but what was there to say?

"I assure you it was purely coincidental that you both ended up here at the same time. Though you gotta wonder..." Micah glanced up at the ceiling. "If there's something or *someone* bigger afoot here, working in your favor. God works in mysterious ways, you know."

She'd be lying if she said the same thought hadn't crossed her mind at least a dozen times. After her epiphany tonight, she was almost sure of it. Regardless of what forces or fate had led both her and Gage here, Hailey intended to make the best of it, this second chance gifted her. Tomorrow. After she'd had enough sleep to trust herself to think straight and form coherent sentences.

"I see you're well prepared." Hailey sat down again to grab her phone and water bottle to take to her room.

"Yep." Micah settled into the rocker, patting the arms affectionately. "Couldn't miss an opportunity to rock a baby now, could I? Think she'll wake up anytime soon?"

"I don't know. She's a pretty mellow baby. Plus, Lucy said she's still sleeping more than usual, recovering from her surgery."

"No worries." Micah began rocking by himself. "I'm content to wait. This chair and I go way back. We don't mind spending some time together."

"Is it a family heirloom?" Hailey's body wanted to go her room and fall into a coma immediately, but she'd never been able to pass up a story about an antique.

"To Lucy and me, yes. We bought this at a yard sale the first year we were married—shortly before our son was born. Skyler had a lot of ear infections, so we both spent a lot of nights sitting up with him in this rocker."

"I didn't realize you had children." Hailey perched on the edge of the couch, her curiosity definitely piqued now. She'd wondered how Lucy and Micah came to be here and ultra-involved in so many charities. That they weren't your typical couple was an understatement. She hadn't seen many pictures around—other than a few of them as a couple—and wouldn't have ever guessed they were parents.

"Just one son." Micah's smile was wistful. "He was three when he died. The neighbor's car rolled over him. Lucy and I were both in the front yard, working and keeping an eye on him. No one was even in the car." Micah paused, a pained expression creasing his brow. "It was just a freak accident . . . One minute Skyler was laughing, then the next . . ."

"Oh, Micah." Hailey thought of her own nieces and nephew around that age. She wasn't even their parent but couldn't imagine the grief she'd feel if something happened to Riley or Sarah or Ross. Hailey glanced at Amura, then set her phone and water bottle aside and reached down to pick her up. Careful to hold her close, Hailey crossed the room and placed the baby in Micah's arms. "She'll sleep just as well or maybe even better if you hold her."

He nodded. "My thoughts exactly. Thanks."

Hailey stood there a moment, looking down at Micah, witnessing the perfectly natural transformation from laid-back north shore resident to loving father. It was apparent from the way he held Amura that Micah knew his way around babies.

"*You and Lucy* should adopt her," Hailey said. "I mean, have you ever thought about that? About having another child or adopting one?"

His smile was still sad. "All the time. Even today when Lucy brought this little one home, I thought for a second . . ." He shook his head. "It'd be too much for Lucy. She's a mother in other ways—loves those kids at the orphanage to pieces—but always she keeps her relationship with them at a safe distance. She won't allow herself to let go completely and give an individual mother's love to any of them."

"Surely she realizes what she's doing. With her degree and understanding of human nature and—"

"—Of course she does," Micah said. "But that doesn't mean she's able to change it. Like the rest of us struggling along in this world, she's managing the hand she's been dealt as best she can. We could have had more children, but she's afraid to risk it all again. She's afraid that if she did and something happened, she wouldn't ever recover. She barely did last time. It took moving across the ocean and restructuring our entire future before she started to feel like she wanted to live again."

"She gives so much to others," Hailey said.

Micah nodded. "She doesn't feel like she can be a mom again, so she does the next best thing—finds love and gives it wherever she can."

"Everywhere. To everyone."

"I can't ask more of Lucy than that. I loved our son, and I would have loved more children, but I love my wife the most." He cradled his hand behind Amura's head and lifted her to his shoulder. "We have a wonderful life, even if it's different than the one we envisioned when we started out."

"You're both amazing. This place, this program, is amazing. I'm sorry I said I was having just a good week."

"I wasn't too worried. After all, the week's not over." Micah glanced up at her, his usual smile restored. "It's always so great for Lucy and me to witness the changes that occur in those who come here. Almost everyone returns home having learned one universal principle."

"Which is?"

"Something I'd wager you've figured out already or will very soon." He paused and stopped the rocker so he could look directly at her. "Alternate endings can be happy too."

23

Leap of Faith

HAILEY STARED AT the phone in her hand. She was perhaps seconds away from confirming her suspicions about Gage's health—a prospect both terrifying and hopeful at the same time. She didn't want to hear that he was as sick as she feared. But if he was, if the whole reason for breaking their engagement had been some ill-conceived nobleness and wanting to spare her the pain he was soon to go through, missing out on the family they'd planned, and the possibility of losing him, then she had to know. It was the first step to getting Gage back.

For how long? The question that had been haunting her all night reared its head again.

The answer didn't really matter. When you loved someone, you accepted the inevitable terms. Eventually, with all love, there was going to be heartache, loss, separation. She hadn't wanted to think about those things now—what woman did when she was madly in love and planning a lifetime with the man of her dreams—but she acknowledged that they were true. For now, she'd just take things one day at a time, one hour at a time, if necessary. She wanted Gage for as long as she could have him, in whatever state she could have him in.

Hailey found Pauline's number quickly in her favorites, proof of yet one more thing she hadn't done after Gage broke their engagement. His mother *was* still one of her favorite people, so why delete her from that list?

The phone rang three times, then nearly a fourth before Pauline answered.

"Hello, Hailey. This is a pleasant surprise." Her voice sounded wary nonetheless.

"Merry Christmas, Pauline," Hailey said, feeling at once comforted at hearing her would-be—and still perhaps might be—mother-in-law. "How are you?"

"Well," Pauline said. "Though a little lonely this year. And you?"

Surprisingly good. "Better than I thought I'd be a few weeks ago." Hailey took a breath for courage, then plunged ahead. "I'm here in Hawaii—on the same trip as Gage."

"Yes. I know." Pauline sounded the tiniest bit guilty. "He called me the first day to tell me, or rather to accuse me of setting that up."

"Did you?" Hailey hadn't considered this before, but it would certainly explain how they both ended up here.

"No."

There was a pause on the line, and Hailey imagined Pauline shaking her head.

"As much as I'd like to take credit—or avoid it, if need be—I had nothing to do with your both being there. Perhaps it's just a case of great minds thinking alike."

Our like-mindedness. It wouldn't be the first time she and Gage had arrived at the same place, unplanned. Months earlier, when they had been looking to open their own shop, she'd arranged a meeting with a realtor to view the property she and Gage ultimately ended up purchasing. To her surprise that day, during that visit with the realtor, Gage had shown up with a friend of his whom he'd contacted about the same property. They'd burst into laughter upon seeing each other—

on the second floor in the room that was to be their eventual bedroom—and agreed right then and there that they'd found the house for both the business and their future family to begin.

"Hailey? Are you still there?" Pauline's voice, filled with motherly concern, carried over the miles and ocean between them.

"Yes. Sorry." Now was not the time to get lost in thoughts of the past. "I'm calling because I'm hoping you can help me. I have a few questions I need answered."

"About Gage?" The uncertainty was back.

"Yes," Hailey said with what she hoped was firm expectation. Pauline would, after all, have to side with her son and owed no explanations to Hailey or anyone else about his actions.

"I promised Gage I wouldn't talk to you about anything."

Hailey had expected as much. "Of course. I understand. I'm not asking you to talk, exactly. I just have three questions, all of which can be answered with a yes or a no. Do you think you could do that?" *Please.* "It's really important."

Pauline's response was several seconds in coming. "I suppose that wouldn't be breaking my promise."

Thank you. Hailey's eyes flickered upward with a silent prayer of gratitude. "Thank you," she said to Pauline. "This means a lot to me—and possibly to Gage as well."

"Have you two talked at all since you've been there?" Pauline asked.

"A little," Hailey said. "I know there's something going on with him, and I have a pretty good idea it has to do with the cancer he had as a child. Can you tell me if I'm right? Does it have to do with the neuroblastoma?"

Another hesitation then, "Yes."

Hailey's heart sank. She'd guessed already, but hearing

his mother confirm made it much more real. Her eyes stung as she asked her second question.

"Is that why he called off our wedding? Why he decided that we shouldn't marry?"

"Yes." Pauline sounded almost relieved to answer.

I knew it. Stupid, stubborn, pig-headed oaf—that I love. The tears overflowed now, sliding down her sunburned cheeks.

"Last question," Hailey promised, smiling in spite of her sorrow and frustration. "If I bought you a plane ticket, could you fly out here the day after Christmas?"

24

It's Not Over Yet

"HAVE FUN TODAY. And get a picture of Charlie taking the first ride on his coaster for me." Brock raised a hand in farewell instead of following Hailey toward the van.

She stopped suddenly and turned on him, nearly running into Ray in the process.

"Sorry," she said as he sidestepped.

"Forget something?" he asked.

"Yeah. My partner." Hands on her hips, Hailey narrowed her eyes at Brock. "What do you mean, have fun and take a picture? You're coming too. You can't abandon us now." She'd thought, after their talk on the beach, that he was over his issues with Charlie and his wheelchair. She hadn't actually seen them together yesterday, since she'd been inside with Amura, but Brock had told her things had gone great when she'd asked him last night at dinner.

"Don't think of it as abandonment," Brock said, hand to his heart as if she'd wounded him. "I'm going to Honolulu this morning to meet with a doctor."

"Oh." She'd done it again, jumping to a conclusion and jumping down his throat. "Is everything all right?"

"Never better—really," he added as her brows rose skeptically. "No need to worry. Plus, I have a suggestion for my replacement. I hear he's hardworking—has experience renovating old houses into design stores or something." Brock stepped closer and lowered his voice. "Plus, you two might have a few things to talk about—if the rumors I've heard are true."

Gage. Hailey looked past Brock to see him coming out the door. He hadn't left yet then. There was still time to put her plan into action. His limp seemed better, but he definitely wasn't moving at full speed.

Bone cancer? In his leg? She wished she knew the details so her mind would quit coming up with so many bad ones.

"Have a great day." Brock waved as he turned away, and then Gage was there, in his place, standing close enough that she could touch him.

One step. Just one and she could be in his arms. *Not yet.* She had to do this right. Carefully.

The others were already in the van, but she and Gage stood awkwardly facing each other for a few seconds. "Hi." They both spoke and then stopped at once.

"I was wondering if you wouldn't mind helping me today," she said hurriedly, before he could move. "Brock has a doctor's appointment in Honolulu, and there's a lot of work left on our project."

"Sure. I think we're all helping finish up what's left anyway, aren't we?" Gage wouldn't quite meet her eye.

Oh yeah. She'd forgotten about that. Maybe there would still be opportunity for her and Gage to work alone. Hailey nodded and clasped her hands together to keep from reaching for him. "Thanks."

He shrugged. "Sure. We've got to finish this playground for these kids. I committed to that when I agreed to come."

"Right." His mom had arranged this trip for him. *Bless her.*

The only seats left in the van were in the very back, and from the sly-to-smug looks she got from Meghan and the others as they climbed in, Hailey guessed that was on purpose. She scooted over to the far one, beside the window, happily anticipating having Gage sitting beside her on the ride over and wondering what his reaction might be if, without saying a word, she reached for his hand.

But instead of taking the seat beside her, he kept to the other side, leaving a space between them.

There's an extra. Brock's not coming. She'd blown that opportunity. But remembering how she'd wanted some space herself, on the flight over, Hailey couldn't fault Gage's choice. Instead of trying to start a conversation here, with so many other ears attuned to them, she spent the drive enjoying the beautiful scenery and her newfound peace, and thinking carefully through everything that had to be done to put her plan into action.

At the orphanage any hope she'd had of being alone with Gage was thwarted yet again. Not only was Charlie assigned to help them, but so were Meghan, Darren, Lisbeth and everyone else who had already finished their projects. Still, it seemed that everyone was on her side and guessed something was up—no doubt Hailey had Meghan to thank—and they all conspired to have her and Gage work closely together as much as possible.

"We'll lay the boards. You two come behind and thread the chain." From Meghan.

"Why don't you and Gage go to the other end of the bridge and work your way toward us. We might go faster with two teams." From Darren a while later, shortly after Meghan had spoken with him.

Hailey and Gage ended up at the far side of the bridge most of the day, laying the track, as it were—tongue-and-groove decking threaded through heavy chain—that made up the floor of the coaster.

"I've been thinking about what you said yesterday." Hailey finally spoke, having gathered her courage and collected her thoughts as much as they could be for a starting point. "If our situations were reversed—"

"Look, Gage! Look at me swing!"

They both turned to see a little girl moving back and forth with jerky movements on the porch swing of the new playhouse.

"That's great, Aimee," Gage called. He looked at Hailey. "I think she wants me to come see her."

"I think so too," Hailey agreed, unable to begrudge the pig-tailed cherub interrupting them.

"Be back shortly." He set his end of the chain down and walked toward the playhouse.

"Could have invited me to come too." Hailey sighed and blew a piece of hair out of her face, then picked up the next board.

Gage was gone for several minutes, and when he returned Ray had joined them, taking over Gage's task beside her.

At four in the afternoon the last of the playground bark had been spread, and the chair coaster and other equipment were finally complete.

Hailey held up her phone, finger hovering, ready to film Charlie's first epic ride. "I'm so excited for him," she said to Gage, who'd only become more sullen and quiet as the day wore on. He'd worked as hard as any of them today, and she worried he wasn't feeling well, that the physical labor was too much on top of whatever was wrong with him.

She hit record as Charlie positioned his chair at the base of the long ramp, then cranked the wheels as fast as he could up the incline. Twice it seemed he might need the help of the pulley system after all, as the chair seemed to stop and almost roll backward, but he kept going, body bent forward, lips pursed, eyes on the goal.

Hailey let out a sigh of relief when he reached the top.

"It's not over yet," Gage said, eyes fixed on Charlie.

She knew what he was talking about, and it wasn't their relationship. Still, she couldn't resist. "You're absolutely right."

Gage shook his head. "That thing looks crazy-dangerous. I can't quite believe Micah and Lucy signed off on this."

"I think Micah would sign off on a lot of things." She recalled his comment about swimming with sharks. "Brock said the engineering is sound. He looked over the plans pretty thoroughly the other day. And you saw how it's put together. Solid."

"Solid or not, Charlie's going to go fast."

Really fast. Hailey held her breath as Charlie gave them the thumbs up, then rolled forward and started down the first drop, accelerating quickly. The chains along the sides and the upturned ridge along the edges were such that his chair could only go forward and wouldn't veer off the track, but she worried he'd get going so fast that he'd be thrown out of his chair head first.

Instead he leaned back, hands pressed to the arms, as he let out a whoop. His already untamed locks blew about wildly, and his shouts of joy rose with each consecutive surge of speed, until the last, smallest hill that set him gently on the long straightaway at the opposite end of the playground. Hailey and Gage hurried to greet him.

"That was great!" Charlie held his hand out for a high five as he rolled past.

They returned the gesture, slapping his palm as he came by. She turned to Gage, hand still up.

"Nice job, partner." She smiled, so happy that they'd worked on this together and that Charlie was so pleased with the result.

Reflexively, it seemed, Gage's hand met hers. After a brief tap, Hailey's fingers began to twine through his, as had been their habit in the past. But Gage didn't react as usual. Instead, he pulled his hand away, leaving hers awkwardly in the air until she tucked it quickly behind her back.

No matter, she told herself as he turned away. He still thought things were over between them. Until he realized they weren't, that nothing in the way of an illness or inability was going to change her mind about loving him, he was likely to keep acting this way. Somehow, she just had to get through.

25

Santa is Polynesian

THE VOLUME ON the portable speaker went up and down, up and down, so that every other reindeer name was alternately shouted at full volume or turned so low you couldn't hear it as two small boys fought over the dial. Chaos and sticky fingers reigned in this most surreal production of Christmas cookies Gage had ever experienced. Even Hailey's parents' house, when all the kids and grandkids were there, was tame comparatively.

"I want to make Santa's beard." Aimee thrust a tube of brown frosting at Gage. "Help me."

"Please," Lucy reminded her as she swept by their table, Amura balanced on her hip. "If we want people to help us and to play with us, we have to use nice words."

"Please, help me," Aimee said, looking up at Gage with a hopeful face that would melt any heart. He lifted her onto his lap.

"All right. I think we should make circles. I bet that will look like Santa's beard. Also, we should probably choose a different color. How about white?"

"Brown," Aimee insisted.

"Your cookie, your call." Gage wrapped his hand over her little one that held the frosting tube.

Across the room, during a low-volume moment, he heard Hailey laugh but forced himself to keep his head down this time. *Good for her for finding some happiness here this week.*

Especially tonight, Christmas Eve, when he knew he'd hurt her again yesterday and then again, a short while ago, when he'd pulled his hand from hers and walked away. Hailey's hopeful expression had almost broken his resolve. It was wreaking more havoc on him than the kids were on this kitchen. He had to get out of here. Tonight. Christmas alone in Waikiki was going to be lousy but better than facing the constant reminder that he couldn't be with Hailey.

Three days from now she would have been my wife. Their wedding had been set for December 27th, so all of her family could be in town for it. Now they were all there without her, and here he was, set to run out on her again.

The Christmas music switched off suddenly, replaced by the sound of a live ukulele playing "Mele Kalikimaka."

"Santa!" Aimee exclaimed.

Gage looked up to see Santa—or a Polynesian version of him, at least—squeezing his large belly through the kitchen door. He had a somewhat well-used, faded red sack slung over his shoulder, and his beard and skin were definitely brown, but the kids didn't seem to mind. Instead of a ho-ho-ho greeting, he strolled about the kitchen, playing his ukulele and singing.

"See." Aimee pointed to his beard. "Brown."

"Yep." Gage guided her hand over the cookie. It made sense to him. After all, most of these kids were some shade of brown. Why shouldn't Santa be too?

"Hello." Hailey sat down beside him, a courageous smile on her beautiful face.

He could tell that she wanted to talk. She'd tried a few

different times today, but always there had been someone or something there to interrupt—thankfully. Gage wasn't sure how much longer he could hold on, or hold out when he really felt like taking her in his arms, kissing her soundly, and begging her to take him back—and to accept the unthinkable.

That would be unthinkable. If he truly loved her like he professed he did.

"What a fine job you're doing on that cookie." Hailey bent her head closer to Aimee's, trying to engage her.

Aimee didn't even look up.

"She's a little focused right now," Gage said gently.

"I can see that." Hailey leaned back, looking perfectly content as she watched the two of them. "I imagine this is what my family is doing right about now too."

He couldn't help it; he looked up at her. "Probably." He remembered last year when they'd made cookies for Santa at her house. It had been a new tradition for him. With just him and Mom at home, there'd been no need for pretense. Each knew where their present came from and who bought it, and usually what it was, long before Christmas.

"You have flour on your nose," Gage said, grateful his fingers were busy so they couldn't reach out to brush it away.

"So I've been told." She made no move to do anything about it. "I'm a messy baker."

That was true. It was also true that against her sunburned cheeks and red hair, that touch of white was particularly charming.

"I know you're busy now, but I was hoping we could talk for a few minutes tonight."

"We talked yesterday, Hailey." *Stay strong.*

She shook her head. "Mostly you talked and I listened. I'd like a turn now. Please," she added, as if she'd overheard Lucy's reminder.

"There's nothing more to say. Nothing you *could* say that will change anything. Besides, I'm leaving right after this."

"Tonight?" Her face fell, hope sliding into panic.

"Yeah. I've got an Uber scheduled to come get me as soon as we're back." That much was true. He was due for his second rabies shot tonight. He supposed he could just leave from the hospital, make a clean break and be gone. "I need to get home to be with my mom for Christmas."

Hailey opened her mouth, and for a second he thought she was going to call him out on his lie. He'd never been any good at them. Instead she pressed her lips together and gave a brief nod. "I see. Tell her I said, Merry Christmas."

"I will."

She rose from the table and walked away, straight through the kitchen and out the door. He caught a glimpse of her as she crossed in front of the window, hand held to her mouth, head bent, and crying.

26

Hail Mary

"I NEED A favor."

"Missed me, did you?" Brock opened the door to his bungalow wider and beckoned Hailey inside.

"Terribly," she said. "Actually, I really did miss you. I wish you could have seen Charlie that first time. I'll tell you all about it later." She glanced out the window. "Right now I need you to do something for me."

"Sure. Anything. Well, maybe. I've kind of got this thing going with Lisbeth now, so I'd better retract my earlier offer for a Hawaiian affair. Sorry."

"You'd better tell me about that later too." Hailey handed him the envelope with Gage's name on it. "Gage is leaving, and I need you to give this to him before he goes."

"He is? What? Things didn't go well for you two today?" The teasing left Brock's voice. He looked at her closer. "You've been crying."

She ignored both his question and his observation. "It's really, really important he gets this. My engagement ring is inside, along with a note."

"Why don't you give it to him yourself?" Brock ran his fingers along the envelope, feeling the bump.

"I don't think he'll listen. I tried talking to him this

afternoon, and he shut me down. I'm already a train wreck. He's leaving in just a minute, and I really don't want to fall apart in front of him." She'd considered that option—wondered if it might be enough to shake Gage from his state of detachment. This week she'd seen him waver, almost cross the line, returning to the man he used to be, but then always he stayed the course. Falling apart in front of him didn't seem her best chance. Really, there was only one. And very likely, it wasn't going to work. But at least she'd know she had tried.

The sound of a door closing, followed by wheels rolling, came from outside.

"Here he comes." Hailey pushed Brock toward the door. "I'll wait here."

She crouched below the window, grateful, for once, that the slats didn't close entirely. She'd be able to hear the exchange. Maybe she could even watch. She peeked through the bottom slats.

"Hey," Brock said. "I hear you're leaving paradise early."

"Yeah." Gage sounded surprised that anyone knew.

"I've been asked to give this to you. I think there's something pretty important inside. I'd take a look at it before you get on any plane."

"Thanks." There was a pause, and Hailey sank to the floor, relieved Gage at least had her note. It wasn't the conversation she'd hoped to have, but a desperate Hail Mary at the eleventh hour. His mom and her parents would be here in less than *forty-eight* hours. Last night she'd felt so much peace, and this morning she'd been so certain about everything. Now she really hoped they were coming for more than an unplanned, last-minute vacation.

"You and Hailey—hit it off pretty well?" Gage asked.

"Saw us on the beach a couple nights ago, did you?" Brock said, sounding like the braggart he'd been that first day.

Hailey grabbed the doorknob and scrambled to her feet, ready to strangle him.

"Yeah. I did. You'd better treat her—"

"Then you should know she flat-out refused me." Brock's tone switched to dead serious. "She's in love with *you*."

Hailey sagged against the door.

"You know why I can't marry her."

"I know you're an idiot," Brock said. "A fool for walking away from an incredible woman. In spite of what you say, this whole thing has nothing to do with you wanting to spare her grief and everything to do with you not feeling like a man anymore. I get it, believe me. At least you're gonna have use of your legs."

"Legs aren't going to give Hailey the life she's dreamed of."

Oh, Gage. Hailey peeked through the window.

"She dreams about you—or the guy you used to be, anyway. I doubt she likes you a whole lot right now."

"Better for her if she doesn't," Gage growled and started forward again.

Brock stepped in front of him, blocking the way. "Yeah, you're probably right. One thing I've learned from Hailey—honesty is really important. She appreciates it more than just about anything. Once I opened up to her about my illness, told her what was wrong with me, she liked me a whole lot more."

"Good for you," Gage said. "But I doubt you'd ask her to marry you, knowing what your future holds."

"I wouldn't ask, Hailey, no." Brock shook his head. "But I'd ask another woman—if I found the right one, if we shared that kind of love. I'd ask because I'd stick by her side if the situation were reversed. Wouldn't you do that for Hailey?"

"Of course," Gage said.

"Well, then." Brock threw up his hands as if that

explained everything. "Love is the best life has to offer, but it never comes with a guarantee. There's no given that once you've found the one, you both live happily ever after or even grow old together. Life doesn't come with a guarantee either, but I wouldn't have passed up a chance to live—even knowing what my future holds and the way things are going to end."

"My ride's here. I've got to go," Gage said.

This time Brock stepped aside, allowing him to pass, but throwing in a parting shot. "Swallow your pride and talk to Hailey. Win her back before it's too late."

Two sets of feet stomped off, followed a minute later by the sound of a car door closing. Hailey ran out of Brock's room in time to see the back of Gage's head in an unfamiliar car as it drove away.

Brock returned, running actually, in that somewhat odd way of his that she now recognized as part of his struggle with MD. He had Allyson in tow. She took one look at Hailey and held her arms out. Hailey fell into them and had the breakdown that had been threatening since the first night she was here.

Her Christmas Eve list was hard. Hailey didn't have her notebook again, she had a migraine from crying—she'd actually made herself sick enough that she'd thrown up earlier—and she wasn't feeling particularly grateful about anything. But she was afraid she'd feel worse if she didn't take a few minutes to find *something* to be grateful for. *Lucy promised this would make me feel better.*

Hailey walked Amura up and down the lanai, trying to soothe both their troubles, and decided it would be all right to *think* her list tonight instead.

Number one. I'm grateful we finished the playground and the kids had so much fun on it.

Two. I'm grateful for the new friends I've made this week. Brock, Lisbeth, Allyson, Meghan, Darren, Caleb, Kirsten, Ray, Lucy, and Micah. They'd all been so kind to her tonight. Everyone knew her situation now, and no one thought it was petty or her problems any less difficult than theirs. They'd shown so much kindness, so much love. She did feel a tiny bit better just thinking about it.

Three. I'm grateful I have Amura to take care of, to distract me. Hailey had been both incredulous and even a little grumpy when Lucy had asked her to take one of the night shifts again, telling Hailey that she was the one who most needed Amura's company.

Amura was still wide awake, chomping on her fist, trying to soothe her swollen gums, and it was nearing midnight. Hailey had found that the only thing that really calmed Amura was walking, out here where the cool breeze could reach them and the ocean was visible below.

Amura's eyes were large as she took in the moon shining on the water. Her legs were busily kicking, while drool pooled on Hailey's arm. *I'm grateful I'm not teething.* She wondered if that was good enough to count.

Four. I'm grateful it's so beautiful here. Someday Hailey hoped she wouldn't recall this trip with sadness. She hoped the happy memories would stand out—her new friends, the children, the turtles, the rain and Christmas carols and beautiful tree—while the sad ones faded away. She was glad to have come, no matter how much she was hurting right now.

And she was. She did. Everything. It hurt to breathe, to think, to move. She'd been hoping for a Christmas miracle, but Gage was gone. *Really gone.* He'd had plenty of time to read her note and come back. But he hadn't. *He isn't.*

Hailey held Amura a little more tightly and bent her head to the baby's as the tears started again. She couldn't be grateful he was here anymore. Only one thing offered potential comfort.

I'm grateful my mom will be here the day after tomorrow.

27

Good will toward men

THE WAY HAILEY saw it there were two courses of action she could take on Christmas Day.

The first was a self-indulgent pity party and denial of reality. She could do some serious crying like she had last night—she imagined the evidence was still visible in the puffiness beneath her eyes—and feel melancholy thinking about her family all at home without her. She could imagine the nieces and nephews dog-piling on top of her, the heavenly aroma of her mom's made-from-scratch cinnamon rolls, the sound of carols being pounded on the perpetually out-of-tune piano. She could imagine Gage.

He would have been beside her, of course. Hailey knew all too well the looks they would have exchanged throughout the day, and the way they would have touched at every opportunity. With only two days until their wedding, it would have been Christmas euphoria.

Door number one was enticing, if only for the possibility of a few minutes of fantasizing how her day should have been.

The second option was to put a smile on her face—even if it was fake—forget about herself, and try to make someone else's day better. Or, in this case, a few people's days better. She could begin with the tiny, wiggly one at her side, the one who had caused Hailey's arm to go numb from being wrapped protectively around her much of the night. Micah had never shown for his middle-of-the-night shift, and Amura hadn't been the happiest of babies at two, three, and four this morning, with those emerging teeth still bothering her.

Hailey opened her eyes to see Amura's brown ones staring at her. The instant they made contact, a huge smile spread across Amura's face, and her legs began churning, kicking Hailey in the stomach.

"All right then," Hailey said, finding her own smile come easily at the sight of Amura's. "Door number two it is. If you can be happy about your life, I can find joy in mine." *Somewhere.*

Where was Gage right now? Had he caught a flight home last night? Had Pauline cancelled her flight tomorrow? For Gage's sake, Hailey hoped so. She didn't want to think of him alone in a hotel on Christmas, and she really didn't want him to find out his mom was supposed to fly to Hawaii for a wedding that wasn't happening now.

She sat up on the sofa in the great room and stretched, then shook out her numb arm. "Your turn." Hailey picked up Amura and held onto her while the baby stood and then bounced on Hailey's lap. When they'd both had a minute to work out the kinks from sleeping on the sofa, Hailey stood and carried Amura into the still-dark kitchen. She flipped on a light and started a bottle sterilizing in a pan of water on the stove, then returned to the great room to change Amura's diaper.

The giant tree loomed over them, lights twinkling, ornaments glistening. *A beautiful tree for a beautiful house on a beautiful island.* But it wasn't home. Hailey felt emotion rising in her throat and fought to keep it back. She was done with tears. For today, at least. She'd think of others and their happiness. She'd do everything she possibly could for everyone else today. She'd make herself as busy as Lucy so there was no time to feel sad or sorry for herself.

Amura in her arms, Hailey stood and looked up at the tree again, the brilliant star on top reminding her of the wise men who had followed the new star to bring gifts to the Christ child. Surely they had not been thinking of themselves or their own comfort as they trekked across the desert for who knows how long, seeking the Savior. Nor had they been thinking of themselves when they heeded God's warning and returned home another way, ignoring Herod's summons.

Another way. That's what I have to do now. Change direction, but move forward all the same.

The peace Hailey had felt two nights before returned, washing over her gently. "I can do this," she whispered. "*We* can do this." She kissed Amura's head, then returned to the kitchen.

In the next half hour she fed Amura, started the store-bought cinnamon rolls rising in the oven, and made orange juice. Toting Amura on her hip, Hailey one-handedly set the long table in the lanai with the Christmas paper plates and cups that Lucy had bought for the orphanage children to use when they came over for breakfast and presents later this morning.

After checking that the rolls were ready, Hailey turned the oven to bake, then decided to help Amura open a present early so she'd have something cute to wear today.

"Help me!"

Hailey's head snapped up. She ran to the window that looked out to the drive, but she couldn't see anything—anyone. It was still too dark.

The shout came again, a man's voice and even more urgent, followed by a loud splash.

The pool. Hailey hurried into the other room, deposited Amura in her portacrib, then ran outside.

In the dim light a head bobbed above the surface of the pool.

"Ray!"

His body moved awkwardly through the water, towing—

"Caleb." *Oh no.* Hailey crossed the deck and plunged into the pool, meeting Ray on the second step. Together they pulled Caleb's motionless body from the water.

"Roll him on his side." Ray pushed Caleb away from him, then pounded on the man's back until a stream of water spilled from his mouth and nose. They flipped Caleb on his back, and Ray leaned over him, ear close to Caleb's mouth.

"Breathing?" Hailey asked.

"Not yet." Ray began CPR.

Allyson's door opened, the light from the room shining behind her as she stood in the doorway. "Call an ambulance!" Hailey shouted.

"Lucy just did." Micah sprinted toward them.

"What else do you need? What can I do?" Hailey asked Caleb, her calm voice belying an internal surge of chaotic emotion. She felt helpless in a situation that demanded action.

Ray's hands were on Caleb's chest, pumping up and down over his heart. With each thrust drops of water squeezed from Caleb's shirt, sliding to the wet pavement.

"I'll get towels." She stood and nearly bumped into Micah.

"Breathe!" Ray shouted. "*Come on*, Caleb. Breathe!"

"What happened?" Allyson came up on Hailey's right while Kirsten, Meghan, and Lisbeth crowded behind them. Darren stumbled out of his room. Brock stood in his doorway, looking disoriented.

"Help me search Caleb's room," Lucy shouted. "If he's

taken something we need to know before the paramedics get here."

Ray and Micah continued working over Caleb while the women hurried to follow Lucy. They converged on the open door to Caleb's room. By the time Hailey entered, Darren was coming out of the bathroom, an empty pill bottle in his hand.

"Found this."

Lucy snatched it and glanced at the label as she ran outside. The wail of a siren filled the air. A baby's faint cry followed.

Amura. Hailey ran toward the main house.

"He's breathing." Micah's hoarse shout came from the pool.

Hailey glanced over her shoulder and saw Ray still bent over, performing CPR. An ambulance screeched into the circular drive, its lights and siren piercing the dark.

In a surreal haze Hailey entered the house, scooped up the crying baby, and held her close.

"It's going to be all right," Hailey whispered, uncertain who she was trying to reassure. From the doorway she watched as the paramedics took over for Ray, hooking Caleb up to an IV and other equipment before putting him on a gurney and loading him into the back of the ambulance.

Micah grabbed Lucy's hand as she started to follow. "I'll go."

"No. I will." Before they could stop him, Ray hopped into the back of the ambulance.

"I'll follow." Micah took the bottle from Lucy, then pulled her into his arms for a brief moment. "Caleb's still with us. He's going to be okay." Micah pressed a kiss to her forehead, then hopped in the jeep and drove off after the ambulance.

Everyone else stood scattered around the yard, shock visible in each face. Lucy ran a hand over her eyes and bent her head forward. "I should have watched him more carefully. I recognized the signs. He told me he was all right, but I should have known he wasn't."

Allyson wrapped an arm around her.

"We just had a session last night," Lucy continued. "I should have realized Caleb seemed happier because he'd decided to check out. People who are suffering depression like he is don't get better at Christmas. They get worse. I shouldn't have let him be alone."

"Personal choice," Allyson said quietly. "Remember what you taught me about that? We all have agency—something none of us can control in another person. Sometimes people do things that hurt themselves and others. Blaming ourselves for their actions doesn't help them or us, or make anything better."

"I don't blame myself—entirely." Lucy sounded weary and older . . . much, much older than she had seemed to Hailey all week. "But if I could have stopped him—"

"Maybe you could have." Allyson steered Lucy toward the house. "For a little while. But what if he'd tried this at home, when there wasn't anyone around to care? Maybe Caleb made the decision to act here, because subconsciously, he knew he was surrounded by people who *do* care about him. You did all you could, Lucy. You've been trying to help him all week. Ultimately, Caleb is still in charge of his actions."

Now who's the therapist? Allyson would excel at that profession, Hailey thought. *Maybe I should encourage her to go back to school.*

"I'm glad to know someone listened," Lucy said half-heartedly.

"We've all been listening," Meghan said as she walked over to her. "I was so angry when I arrived—furious at my parents and the world. You helped me see I was being as ridiculous as they are and that anger isn't going to help anyone. You've helped all of us so much this week."

Amen. Hailey thought about how applicable the personal choice talk was to her situation as well. She'd done everything she could think of to reach Gage, but she hadn't been able to change his mind or make him confide in her. *I couldn't keep him.*

Just as Allyson hadn't been able to keep her husband from straying and Lucy hadn't been able to keep Caleb from hurting himself.

There's so little we can *control.* It was enough to make a planner and control freak like herself crazy. Hailey stepped aside as Allyson guided Lucy into the house and the others filed in behind.

"Are you baking something?" Kirsten asked hopefully, sniffing the air.

The rolls. "Oh my goodness. Yes. Hold Amura, please." Hailey handed Amura off to Kirsten, then went to check the cinnamon rolls. She discovered her hand was trembling as she opened the oven door. *Did Caleb really just try to take his life?*

Please don't let the rolls be burned. Two completely incongruent thoughts. She felt so exhausted and overwhelmed. Frazzled, before the day even started. How was she supposed to keep her resolve to be positive today?

Would anyone even want breakfast now? How were they supposed to celebrate Christmas, to carry on as if nothing had happened?

And the children . . . Hailey groaned. How were they supposed to be happy and cheerful and make Christmas wonderful for all the orphanage kids?

She pulled the pan out and set it on the counter, feeling some small relief that the rolls were okay. Resting both hands on the island, she leaned forward, taking a minute to pull herself together.

Let Caleb be all right. She'd only known him a few days and had probably spent the least amount of time with him, out of all the guests here this week, but she hurt for him just the same. *To be in such a dark place that he'd think of ending everything.*

She'd been in a pretty dark place herself, too, this past month, but nothing like Caleb's. Yet one more realization of how blessed she truly was.

Hailey drizzled frosting over the rolls and thought about that, about what a balm gratitude had become to her heart in such a short time.

By the time she finished frosting the rolls and returned to the great room, she felt slightly better—less like she might throw up and collapse on the floor and sob uncontrollably again. She'd had her turn for a breakdown last night, and she was glad an emotional fit was the worst she'd done. Even so, she was through with that behavior. Period. If nothing else, she needed to have her junk together for Lucy. The poor woman had worked so hard helping all of them, and right now she seemed so discouraged.

It was five minutes to seven when Darren went to the piano and began playing a Christmas hymn as melancholy as the occasion. His rich voice accompanied his fingers as they rolled over the sullen notes on the keyboard. "I Heard the Bells on Christmas Day."

Hailey took Amura from Kirsten and went to stand near the piano, where she swayed slowly to the music, holding Amura close while the baby continued to slurp on her fist.

Darren's voice was mesmerizing, and the lyrics held her spellbound as well. They were sad, each verse more hopeless than the previous, yet always the last line sang of peace on earth, good will to men.

Hailey felt her own head bow with despair when she

thought of Caleb on his way to the hospital and Gage spending Christmas alone. This was supposed to be a Christmas she'd never forget. That much was true, but for all the wrong reasons.

Darren played an interlude between verses, his fingers marching up the keys in a crescendo before he began a verse that started differently, the lyrics building in their own way. "Then pealed the bells more loud and deep," Darren sang, "God is not dead, nor doth He sleep."

Lucy joined in. "The wrong shall fail, the right prevail with peace on earth, good will to men."

"Thank you, Darren." Lucy placed a hand on his shoulder in a motherly way. "I needed that."

"We all did. Just like good old Henry when he wrote the original poem." Looking around the room, Darren asked. "Everyone knows that story, right?"

Brock and Lisbeth shook their heads.

"Tell us," Allyson said, giving Darren an encouraging smile.

"All right." He stood and moved away from the piano. They all migrated toward the sofa with him.

"Henry Wadsworth Longfellow wrote it, during a terrible time in his life." Darren sat on the edge of the hearth, facing the rest of them. They were down four now, and the happiness and laughter that had filled this room just a day ago seemed to have permanently fled.

"Longfellow was a family man," Darren began. "I think I always liked this story because of that," he added, as an aside. "An English teacher shared it with me some years ago, and I admit to feeling jealous, because my parents had never shown the kind of caring and concern that Longfellow did for his family."

"You can have a family like that yourself, someday," Lucy

reminded him. "None of us have to repeat the past or be anything like what we've come from."

Unless we want to. Hailey had never loved or missed her parents more than she had the last few days. She couldn't think of anything better than being as much like her mom as possible.

Darren cleared his throat, then began the story again. "Longfellow was married to a woman named Fannie Appleton. They were the parents of six children. One died as an infant."

From the corner of her eye, Hailey glanced at Lucy, noting the subtle flash of pain that crossed her face.

Empathy. Lucy didn't have to imagine what it was like to lose a child.

Darren continued. "Less than two years before he wrote 'I Heard the Bells,' Fannie died a horrific death when her dress caught on fire. Henry was at home when it happened, and he tried to put out the flames. Fannie died from her injuries. Henry's burns were so severe that he was unable to attend her funeral." Darren paused. "Fannie was his second wife to die. His first, Mary, had died after a miscarriage."

"*Twice*," Kirsten murmured. "He had to live through it twice."

Darren nodded. "Both times his grief was said to have been tremendous. So unfair. He loved each of his wives and lost them both. How many other people don't love their spouses, wouldn't care if something happened to them—but nothing does."

From the look on Darren's face it was easy to guess he was thinking about his own parents.

Darren rubbed a hand across his chin. "Henry grew a beard to cover the scars on his face, but that couldn't disguise his grief, which was said to have been so intense that he feared he would be put in an asylum."

"Is this story supposed to cheer us up?" Brock asked with a false laugh.

Hailey glanced over and noticed how close he and Lisbeth were sitting on the sofa, their hands ever-so-casually touching. *That* cheered her up. Hailey smiled. If ever two people needed a little friendship and love and joy in their lives . . .

"Let Darren finish the story," Allyson encouraged.

"In 1863 Henry's oldest son had enlisted in the army, fighting for the union. In late November he was shot, an injury that nearly took his life. When Henry received word in early December he traveled immediately to see his son and was given grave news upon his arrival. The injury might result in paralysis. It didn't," Darren added quickly at Brock's increasing frown.

"On a bleak Christmas day, when the country was at war with itself, he had lost his love and nearly his son, and the future must have seemed dismal, Longfellow wrote his despair in the words of his poem—later turned hymn. But even in the midst of all the tragedy that surrounded him, he remembered there was good in the world. He was able to find at least a glimpse of it and remind us that we all have reason to hope. 'The wrong shall fail, the right prevail, with peace on earth, good will to men.'"

"Beautifully said." Allyson beamed at him, and Hailey had a split second to wonder if someday, in the future, there might be something between those two.

After returning her warm smile with one of his own, Darren leaned forward, elbows braced on his knees as his hands moved animatedly. "I've always loved that story and the song. When I first heard it in high school, I was in the thick of some really awful years with my family. I hadn't any reason to believe that life would ever get better. But I read Longfellow's poem and learned about his life, and it gave me hope. I wasn't the only one who'd gone through terrible things, and I wouldn't be the only one to come out of them."

"You're all going to come out of them." Lucy looked up from the phone clasped in her hands. "Even Caleb. Micah just sent a text. Caleb's stable. Ray found him in time. He'll be all right." She leaned her head back against the sofa cushion and expelled a great breath. "Today we were lucky."

"Today we were blessed," Hailey said.

Lucy looked over at her and smiled. "We *were* blessed."

28

The Joy of Giving

"GOOD MORNING. MERRY Christmas, everyone." Micah's voice lacked some of its usual enthusiasm, and the dark circles beneath his eyes made it appear he'd had even less sleep than Hailey, even before the pool scare. He stepped into the great room and almost immediately collapsed on the sofa.

Along with the others, Hailey drifted toward him, eager to hear any news of Caleb. It was nine. Micah had been at the hospital nearly two hours.

"Caleb is as good as can be expected," Micah said. "I can't share any specifics, but the main thing is he's going to be all right. Ray wanted to stay with him. He said to tell you all he's sorry he's missing Christmas morning with you and the children."

"Ray is truly the bright spot, the reason we had a *miracle* this morning." Lucy swept into the room, her floral dress trailing behind, as she made her way over to Micah. She leaned over the couch, then wrapped her arms around him from behind. "Now we know why Ray needed to be here too."

Lucy looked up at Hailey and the others. "He almost didn't get selected. He didn't fit the usual profile of those we invite to participate in this program."

"He's been a great addition—a great example," Hailey added.

Lucy nodded and straightened, keeping her hands on Micah's shoulders. "And now much more. There is always a lot of thought and prayer that goes into the selection of the participants. It's tough, because we almost always have two or three times the number of applicants to the spots we have available."

"But those who come always end up having a purpose for being here. Sometimes we don't realize what that is—until later." Micah pushed himself off the couch, then walked around to meet Lucy. He kissed her on the cheek, then took her hand in his two, in a display of affection that melted Hailey's heart.

Lucy nodded her agreement. "It's uncanny the miracles we've seen over the years and the almost magical way so many lives have been affected."

"Because we work for the man upstairs." Micah wrapped his arm around Lucy, and they both turned toward the tree. "And now *this* man says it's about time for breakfast and presents—if we want any of either before all those kids get here."

Hailey managed to bury her sorrow enough to actually enjoy sitting with Amura on her lap and helping her open her gifts—or helping her enjoy ripping the wrapping paper and shredding the bows, at least. So far Amura had been only marginally impressed with what was inside.

"Hey, Hailey, catch." Brock threw a lumpy, horribly-wrapped gift her direction. "No negative comments," he said as she caught it and looked at it curiously. "MD makes it hard to wrap presents, too, you know. My fingers—"

"You're so full of it." Lisbeth rolled her eyes. "He's just lazy. I told him he needed to do a better job wrapping."

Hailey tore at the flap sticking out at the end, and the one piece of tape holding the paper together gave way quickly. A rolled T-shirt fell into her lap. She unrolled it, then, laughing, held it up for all to see. A large headshot of Brock covered much of the front with block letters beneath.

THIS IS MY NEW FAVORITE SHIRT

"Told you I'd take care of you." Brock bobbed his head and strutted about, as if he was the coolest kid on the block. "I expect to see you wearing that on next year's Christmas card."

"Of course." Hailey added it to the pile of things for Amura to drool on.

"This one is for Allyson." Micah held up a small box. Hailey smiled.

"Read the note out loud, if you don't mind," Lucy added. "It's beautiful."

"All right." Puzzled, Allyson opened the card—identical to those everyone else would be getting today.

Hailey hadn't purchased something for everyone, but she'd made sure to take the time—before last night, thankfully—to write them all a letter, expressing her admiration and appreciation. She was a better person for having met each of them this week.

Allyson began reading. "A symbol of the moon and imbued with magical properties, the pearl has long been revered as one of the most precious jewels. Not found in the earth, but in the depths of the sea, it is said that wearing a pearl protects a person from fire and dragons—so I would think it should equally protect from a toxic ex-husband and ex-best friend." Allyson paused, swallowed, and began reading again.

"I hope you'll wear this in place of your old ring and remember that *you* are of greater worth than all the pearls in the sea. You've become so to me this week. Thank you for being my friend. Hailey."

Allyson looked up at her. "Thank you. This is too sweet."

"Open it," Hailey said, grinning, feeling a bit like she had the first year she'd given her mom an actual Christmas present in addition to the homemade one from school. Never mind that it had been a pair of knee-high, royal blue *Peanuts* socks. She'd felt so good that morning, when her mother opened them and oohed and aahed over the sparkly socks featuring Linus and Lucy.

This felt just as good, and hopefully she'd done a better job at picking out something Allyson would actually like. Hailey had spent the entire $250 and then some on this ring. She thought it was gorgeous, and she really, really hoped Allyson did too. She needed something on that empty finger, something as amazing as she was.

"Oh, my." Allyson lifted the ring from the box for all to see. "It's so beautiful." She caught Hailey's eye again, over the heads of Lisbeth and Meghan, who'd bent to admire the ring.

Feeling all warm and fuzzy inside, Hailey returned her attention to Amura and handed her a new stuffed giraffe.

"I love it so much." Allyson came over to show off her ring and give Hailey a hug. "You are the *best* friend. I never thought I'd be grateful for my marriage ending—and I'm not, exactly—but I am grateful it led me here, to beautiful people like you."

Micah kept passing out presents. There were a lot—a lot more than Hailey had expected to see. Most were for the children who would be coming over shortly. But it seemed everyone had found their inner Santa and done a little shopping on the sly.

"The second batch of cinnamon rolls are ready," Kirsten announced, carrying a tray from the kitchen. "I've had three already," she said. "You guys better help me out. I can only justify that last one for my mom. Anymore and I'll be sick."

"Over here. We'll take them." Darren held out his hands and took the tray. Brock wasn't far behind.

"No more rolls, then, but try this instead." Hailey handed Kirsten the wrapped box containing the seashell ornament she'd bought at the Hallmark store.

"Another gift? You already made sure I had the rolls."

"Open it," Hailey urged.

Kirsten untied the bow carefully, then, with equal care, began unfolding the paper without tearing it. "We always did this," she said sounding apologetic. "Mom said it was so we could reuse everything, but I think it was just to make Christmas last longer." She pulled out the ornament and held it up for all to see. "Oh, Hailey. It's perfect."

"You needed an ornament this year," Hailey said.

"Never let your traditions die," Lucy added. "When your loved one is gone, they become even more important. As does remembering." She reached up high on the tree and took down an ornament Hailey hadn't seen before. It certainly hadn't been in with the others in the boxes. A simple construction-paper star, formed by tracing a small child's hand at different angles and tied with a piece of yellow yarn, dangled from Lucy's fingers. Once, it had probably been covered with glitter, but now only a few sparkles remained.

"I made this with our little boy the last Christmas he was with us."

Micah came and stood beside Lucy, wrapping his arm around her waist. She leaned into him.

"He's been gone nearly twenty years. I still miss him every single day." Lucy paused, her unflappable composure slipping. "But in his memory we share the love we felt for him. We give it away as copiously as we can, and we count ourselves blessed for the time we had together."

Count yourself blessed. Hailey had been hearing about

gratitude and giving all week, but the importance of both finally sank deep into her soul. She understood now. Lucy did too. She wasn't just talking the talk; she'd lived through real grief and found the path to healing. *And happiness.*

Hailey hugged Amura to her, grateful for this little person to love this morning, grateful for all the nieces and nephews she'd go home to in a couple of days. She wasn't getting married. There was no possibility of her own newborn next Christmas. But she had a family who loved her, and she loved them.

"Lucy and I have a gift for each of you," Micah said.

"Of sorts," Lucy added. "Don't get your hopes up. You know with us, nothing is ever just about you."

Everyone laughed. Hailey wasn't sure how any of them could have possibly missed that lesson this week.

Micah handed out miniature red stockings. Hailey took hers and reached inside, finding a Hawaiian Holidays ornament that featured a picture of the resort in all its beauty, and a wad of cash, rolled and tied with a red ribbon.

"This is your pay-it-forward money," Lucy explained. "Along with the $250 you were given from your payment this week to spend on the children here, this $100 is for you to do good with once you get home."

"And she expects a report from each of you." Micah rested his hand on Lucy's shoulder. "Nothing upsets my wife more than when participants in our program don't stay in touch and let us know how they are doing."

"We hope this gives you a jump start at home, a reason to look for ways to do good—of course, money isn't always the way to accomplish that," Lucy added. Her hand reached up to cover Micah's on her shoulder, and his other arm went around her waist as she leaned against him.

It was good to see their love. Instead of making her feel

sad about her own lack thereof, Hailey felt genuinely happy for them. They'd survived something horrible and had used the experience to do good for so many. *Why can't I do the same?*

She raised her hand. "Can I share what I want to do with my money right now?"

"Of course," Lucy said.

Hailey stood, bringing Amura with her and balancing her on her hip. "When I was at the orphanage the other day, I noticed how plain the dormitory wing is—no offense to either of you." She glanced at Micah and Lucy.

"None taken," Lucy assured her.

"I have several ideas for how to change that. I'd like to design the inside of the orphanage—everything from cheerful murals to bright light fixtures and fun furniture. I could come back some time next year—and possibly bring a volunteer team with me—to complete it."

"I'll come back to work on it with you," Kirsten said.

"Me too," Allyson added.

The others all followed, adding their commitment and enthusiasm. Hailey was excited about this, but even more so about the seed of an idea that had just sprouted in her brain. Why couldn't she do the same thing elsewhere? At other children's institutions, be they orphanages or low-income schools? Daycare centers? At-risk children in low-income housing could probably benefit the most from a change to their environment. What if she followed in Lucy and Micah's footsteps and started a nonprofit, hers aimed at improving living and learning conditions for underprivileged children?

In college she'd taken a class on the correlation between environment and mood. The research was out there, linking mental illnesses like depression and anxiety to negative environments. It would be a matter of finding that research, putting it together, presenting her idea . . .

Her mind was churning now, racing through the many steps she'd have to go through to reach the end product—changing the life of a child for the better. If Joanna Gaines could take the worst house in a neighborhood and make it beautiful, why couldn't she, Hailey Walsh, take the worst classrooms, hospitals, child-care centers, and even bedrooms and make them beautiful? Sometimes a person's environment made all the difference. *I could make that difference.*

An excitement, even greater than when they'd renovated the shop, took hold inside of her. She was going home with a purpose and a plan. An alternate ending, Micah would say. *A good one.*

"I'd like to share what I'm going to do with my money as well."

Everyone's attention turned to Brock, already standing, leaning on the cane Lisbeth had given him for Christmas.

"I'm going to buy a plane ticket today so that next week I can fly up to Portland. I'm going to hold Lisbeth's hand before she goes into surgery, and I'm going to be there when she gets out, when she's talking funny and her eyes are puffy and she's got a giant turban on her head." Brock directed a goofy face at Lisbeth.

"Just so long as you don't fall on top of me with your clumsy walk," she dished right back.

"And then I'm going to keep going to Portland. Every month, every couple of weeks if I can swing it. I'm going to be there when she's getting chemo dripped into her veins, I'm going to hold her when she's crying because her hair is falling out. I'm going to be the friend she can't get rid of, that sticks to her like glue no matter what. And I don't care if it costs me a million dollars in plane tickets. I'm going to have to sell my condo anyway—too many stairs—and I can't think of anything better to do with the money than to be there for her.

Plus—" His teasing smile returned. "If I show up in Portland, Lisbeth will be off the hook with her family about that *friend* she was supposed to be spending Christmas in Hawaii with."

Hailey raised her hands to clap with the others. Brock had come a long way this week. He seemed to be accepting his illness as well as realizing what kind of relationships really mattered. Lisbeth crossed the room and came to stand beside him, first kissing his cheek, then snatching his cane and pretending she was going to whack him on the head with it.

"Thanks for embarrassing me."

"Get used to it. I plan on doing it frequently." Brock wrapped his arm around her.

Another swell of happiness rose within Hailey. It looked like Brock had found his holiday distraction and more. *Good for them.*

"*Normally* we don't condone this kind of behavior in our groups." Lucy attempted a stern expression. "But in this case, I can't help but feel right encouraging it." Her grin broke free.

"Here's another gift for Amura." Meghan handed Hailey a present that wasn't one she'd wrapped. The paper was pink, with white stars and colorful rainbows all over it. "It's from Gage."

Hailey's heart did its triple beat again, just hearing his name.

"I was with him when he bought it. He picked it out himself. He thought that maybe it was something Amura could wear when she meets her new family—if she ends up going to the states where it's colder, that is." Meghan shrugged as if uncomfortable being the messenger. "I'm really sorry he left, Hailey."

"It's all right. We all tried." Hailey blinked to keep the tears she felt from surfacing. She tore open the paper, imagining Gage's hands on it before hers. He'd chosen this, wrapped it. He'd thought of this little girl when she wasn't even his to worry over.

"Oh, how precious," Allyson exclaimed when Hailey lifted the cream-colored knit dress from the box.

"There are booties and a hat to match too." Meghan crouched beside Hailey and held those up for the others to see. Lisbeth, Allyson, and Kirsten all crowded close, admiring the sweet outfit.

Brock elbowed Darren. "You paying attention to this? The way to a woman's heart—baby clothes. They don't teach you that in school."

Still struggling to hold in her tender emotions, Hailey tucked the outfit carefully back inside the box. She'd been doing so well, and now—

Darn you, Gage. He should have been here with her. Or they should have been at home in New York with her family. And if he bought baby clothes, it should have been for their child.

Pushing aside piles of wrapping paper, Darren stood. "I—uh—didn't get gifts for anyone other than Joseph, the little boy assigned to me. Presents never really meant much in my family. Money wasn't an issue, so anything we got wasn't a gift that had meaning attached to it. It was just another thing to own." He put his hands in his pockets and looked down at the gifts still piled beneath the tree. "But you all have shown me more about Christmas and giving this week—and especially this morning—than I learned in the previous twenty-seven years. So while I don't have any*thing* to give to each of you, I'd like to share my gift of music again—if that's all right. I think a few carols right now, before the children come in, and as they get here, might be nice."

"An excellent idea," Lucy said. "Especially since I missed your concert the other night."

Darren went to the piano. "This first one is for you, Lucy and Micah. You've shown me the kind of person I want to be, and what a happy marriage looks like. For that I will always be grateful." He pulled his gaze from them to look around the room. "Feel free to sing if you know the words, though this one is lesser known."

"Sleep, my child, and peace attend thee, all through the night. Guardian angels God will send thee, all through the night . . ."

Hailey glanced at the others, everyone lost in their own thoughts as the gentle music washed over them. If ever there were guardian angels, she felt like she'd met them this week. *As well as having the opportunity to be one myself.* She cuddled Amura as she listened to Darren's tenor.

"While the moon her watch is keeping, all through the night. While the weary world is sleeping, all through the night. O'er thy spirit gently stealing, visions of delight revealing Breathes a pure and holy feeling, all through the night."

The peace I felt, even after I knew Gage was sick. It was hard-earned and still fleeting. She'd yet to hang onto it for terribly long, but Hailey had hope for it, that she'd be able to lasso it and keep it close for longer periods of time going forward.

"Love's young dream, alas, is over,
yet my strains of love shall hover
Near the presence of my lover, all through the night."

Her dreams of a life with Gage were over. *But I do love him still.* Maybe she always would. Hailey hoped fervently, with all her heart, that somehow he would feel her love wherever he was. For the first time since they'd broken up, her heart ached more for him than it did for herself. She would be all right—eventually. But if the things Brock had told Gage yesterday were true, he was hurting in more ways than she could imagine.

"Thou, my love, art heavenward winging, home through the night..."

"Be safe, Gage," Hailey whispered. "Wherever you are. Be happy."

29

He's Got Legs

CAR HORNS SOUNDED outside, followed by doors slamming and the sounds of happy voices.

"Brace yourself, everyone," Micah said. "The wild things are here."

Lucy elbowed him on her way to open the door. "Have you looked at yourself today? Your hair is about the wildest thing I've seen in a long time."

"Good. Someone needs to scare these little monsters into behaving themselves." He rubbed both hands over the top of his head, ruffling his hair even more, then turned to face Hailey and the others. "I really do love these kids. They just tend to be a little hard on the house. And I'm wiped out already."

Hailey knew exactly what he meant, on both counts. Her nieces and nephews had destroyed more than a few things in her parents' home, and given what little sleep she'd had last night and the emotional roller coaster of the last twenty-four hours, she wasn't sure how she'd make it through the day either.

Lucy swung the double doors wide, and the children poured in, several moving somewhat more slowly than normal children. She waved at Charlie, and he waved back but then wheeled his chair over near Brock.

Aimee, the little down syndrome girl Gage had built the playhouse with, looked around, her face upturned in a hopeful sort of way, which soon gave way to pouting when she didn't see Gage.

Right there with you. Hailey was about to go over to her when Meghan spotted Aimee and took her hand and led her to the tree. The faster children began grabbing presents, with no apparent thought as to whose they were. Lucy helped a boy with cerebral palsy cross the threshold, and the orphanage staff followed, pushing those in wheelchairs who needed help.

The room that had seemed so grand now felt as if it might burst. At the piano Darren's version of "Jingle Bells," assisted by a few pairs of hands on either side, didn't sound quite as polished as it had before. He didn't seem to mind but was encouraging his helpers.

Hailey didn't mind either. The chaos reminded her of home, and she drank it in gratefully, until Brock stood up on the fireplace hearth and rang a bell to get everyone's attention.

"I have a special present for Charlie," he began. "It isn't here today, but I'd like to tell you—and him—about it." Brock beckoned Charlie closer, then waited as a path cleared for him to maneuver his chair through.

"Most of you know how smart and fast and strong Charlie is. He doesn't miss much—except having legs." Brock stepped down from the hearth and put his hand on Charlie's shoulder. "I got to thinking that he shouldn't have to miss those either, so I sent a last-minute request to the North Pole and had a chat with some of Santa's helpers. Charlie—" Brock turned so they were facing each other. "How would you like a new pair of legs for Christmas?"

Legs? Could he possibly mean—Hailey tried to make eye contact with Brock, but his attention was all for Charlie.

Charlie's brow furrowed and instead of smiling, he

frowned, displaying the same uncertainty as several other children in the room. "Is this a joke?"

"No joke," Brock said. "Let me show you what I'm talking about." He raised a hand, and Micah dimmed the lights while Lucy and Lisbeth hurried to close the shades.

A picture flickered to life on the wall above the fireplace. Brock left Charlie's side to hit play on his laptop, and a short video began.

It featured a boy who was perhaps a little younger than Charlie. He started on the opposite side of a track from the camera, then ran closer and closer, an exuberant grin on his face. He came close enough that he had to stop, as his face filled the camera frame. Clapping and cheers sounded in the background, and the camera swung to a stand full of people.

"I did it!" the little boy exclaimed. "I ran all the way around by myself."

The camera panned down to the little boy's legs—or where his legs should have been. Instead there was a set of prosthetics, beginning at his knees.

Oh, Brock. This time Hailey did catch his eye and gave him a huge smile. *I could kiss you,* she mouthed.

He opened his eyes, as if shocked, then inclined his head toward Lisbeth.

She probably already had kissed him, Hailey realized, and felt only happiness for them both.

For the rest of the short film Hailey watched Charlie as his disbelief changed to shock and then excitement. Before the video was even over he'd practically vaulted from his wheelchair.

"I'm getting legs!"

Everyone burst into applause. Hailey nearly burst into tears—happy ones. *Legs!* What an amazing gift. She caught Brock's eye once more and smiled. *Nice job, partner.*

30

Misunderstanding

"Fancy meeting you here." His mom wrapped her arms around Gage and held him tight. "Rough Christmas?"

"The worst." He'd spent the night on a chair in the airport, watching happy people on their way to visit loved ones or enjoying long-anticipated reunions. Constant hugging and kissing and joy to remind him of what he'd left behind.

He stepped back from his mom's embrace and took her luggage. "I still can't believe you're here."

"I could say the same about you," she retorted, slipping quickly into scolding-mom mode. "Why aren't you with Hailey?"

"We've been over this," Gage said. "I'm tired of talking about it. I'm really sorry she flew you all the way out here for nothing. But since she did, let's just enjoy our day together, okay? What would you like to see?"

"My future daughter-in-law." His mom stopped walking, right in the middle of pedestrian traffic going either direction.

Gage took her arm and pulled her to the side. "I'm sorry, Mom. I really am. I know you love Hailey. I know you wanted a daughter-in-law and a bunch of grandkids and—"

"Hold it right there." She poked a finger into his chest. "I *never* said anything about wanting grandchildren. That wasn't an expectation of mine." She lowered her hand, letting it slide down to grasp his. "Gage, I'm so sorry you didn't know. I can't help but feel responsible for all of this. I should never have assumed your father told you, back when he gave you the sex talk."

"Truth be told, he didn't actually cover that either." Gage managed a smile at her horrified expression. "But don't worry. I'm good."

"If the man wasn't already dead," she muttered.

"*Mom.*"

She squeezed his hand. "You know I loved your father very much. I still do. But he wasn't always the best at communicating. I'm sorry to say I see a similar trend in you." She linked her hand through his arm, and they started walking again. "I suppose we can trace this problem back to that, to the very beginning, when you were so little and so sick. There were decisions about your care to be made daily. It was overwhelming. We probably didn't have the best doctors or information because we were young and naive. I only knew that we had to do whatever we could to save you.

"I was a mess, so I let your dad talk to the doctors most of the time. He made the decisions. It didn't occur to me until later—too late—that we should have had other concerns—about things that would affect you later in life. At the time we were focused on just one thing—saving your life."

"Don't beat yourself up, Mom. I'm here, aren't I? The picture of health—except for this beat-up leg. Which was my fault." Gage grimaced as he looked down at the large bandage covering his seventeen stitches. "I've never had cancer since. I'm alive and well, thanks to you."

"Exactly." She looked up at him.

A disconcerting view, as far as Gage was concerned.

Wasn't a kid supposed to look *up* to his parents? He had almost a foot on her now.

"You're young and healthy. You have a great career. You're a wonderful person with love to share. You have so much to offer. Just because you can't give Hailey children doesn't mean you can't give her love and a happy life."

"Children are such a big deal in her family. She'd be the anomaly, and she'd hate that. It's where she's at now, as the unmarried and childless one."

"So marry her, and adopt a child later if you want to. There are other ways to be a parent, you know."

"I know." He'd thought through all this a million times it seemed. "It's just not the dream we had. It's so much for her to give up."

"You don't think giving you up hurts her more?" his mom asked gently.

"Maybe. At first. But I think she's made peace with it. On Christmas Eve she gave me back her ring."

"She did?" His mom sounded shocked. "Are you sure, Gage? What did she say when she gave it back?"

"Nothing. It's just in an envelope."

"Let me see." She stopped walking again and held her hand out.

Rather than argue, Gage dug through his backpack to find it. Maybe if his mom understood things were well and truly over she'd leave him alone about this and they could have a nice day—since she'd flown all this way. *On Hailey's dime.* He hated knowing they'd both felt that much hope so recently.

"Here." He handed her the crumpled, sealed envelope.

She tore it open, dropped the ring in her hand, and opened the note inside. Her eyes scanned it, then filled with tears. "Oh no. Hailey thinks—Read this." Mom thrust the note at him.

Gage,
I know you're sick. I know it's serious. I know you can't have children. None of that matters. I just want to be together for what time you have left. I said yes once. I will again. You just have to ask.
Love, Hailey

31

Soaring

HAILEY HELD ONTO the back of the seat in front of her as the sixteen-passenger jeep rumbled over the rough terrain through the jungle. Music from *Moana* piped over the speakers, and she couldn't help but smile, though the sun wasn't up yet and she was shivering again in the pre-dawn mist. She was pretty sure she could check off safari ride through a rainforest from her bucket list—after she added it, of course.

Usually the day after Christmas was a letdown, with the holiday and festivities over and family and friends returning home. Hailey had expected that phenomenon to be present even more so today, their last full day in Hawaii.

She should have known better.

Lucy and Micah were certifiable geniuses, rousing everyone bright and early, once again, for yet another adventure. Thankfully it wasn't swimming with sharks but a day at Kualoa Ranch, beginning with this sunrise jeep expedition.

"Almost there," Micah announced as they roared through a stream and powered up the steep side of a mountain.

There was nothing but green, as far as the eye could see. Lush, oversized leaves reached through the open sides to brush her arm, and enormous trees lined the road and arched overhead. It was easy to see why *Jurassic Park* and many other movies had been filmed here.

Allyson shivered in the seat beside Hailey. Like the rest of them, she looked pretty tired. Christmas afternoon and evening had been crazy and fun and long and exhausting with a houseful of excited children. "Where do you suppose Micah's taking us?"

"There, maybe." Hailey pointed out her side of the open jeep to a picnic area at the top of the rise. Chairs formed a circle on the ground, and a breakfast spread that might actually feed this crowd covered two tables.

"Yes, food!" Across the aisle Ray pumped his fist in the air. He'd rejoined them today, for the morning at least, while Caleb met with doctors and psychiatrists at the hospital.

The jeep crested the hill, then parked. In the semi dark, everyone filed out the back. Hailey noticed Lisbeth helping Brock down the steps instead of the other way around.

Hailey stood in line with the others and loaded up her plate with fruit, eggs, and sweet bread, then sat beside Meghan just as the sun made its appearance, illuminating Oahu's eastern coastline.

Micah pulled the mic from inside the jeep and began telling them the history of the tiny island of Mokolii, or Chinaman's Hat.

"According to local legend, Hiʻaka, the volcano goddess Pele's sister, created the island by slaying a dragon, a noʻo, and setting his huge flukes in the water as a landmark. Later legend tells us that King Kamehameha I used the turtle-shaped Mokapu Peninsula, visible from the island, as a secret underwater tunnel to safely reach Molokai."

Hailey found Hawaii's history fascinating and began dreaming up ideas for the orphanage that would incorporate some of those legends and facts into the décor. Her mind was busy filing ideas away when another rainbow appeared, this one even brighter than the one she'd seen while kayaking. It began in the water and made a perfect arc over Chinaman's Hat, disappearing on the other side.

"How often do you have stunning rainbows like this?" Hailey asked Lucy, who'd come to sit by her.

"All the time," Lucy said. "Admittedly, we're spoiled. They come after the rain and often just before something spectacular happens."

"Like the turtles I saw," Hailey said. "I saw a rainbow that morning before the turtles swam right by me."

"Yes. *Just* like that," Lucy said in a knowing sort of way. She seemed particularly happy this morning. "I've no doubt this rainbow is a sign of something wonderful to come."

"I take it you never miss living on the mainland," Allyson said.

"Oh, of course we do—sometimes," Lucy said. "But we made the conscious choice to come here. Change is always like that. Something is lost or left behind. The trick is to make sure you're trading that for something better, or as better as can be. I would have chosen the opportunity to raise our son over all of this beauty and the experiences we've had here. But we aren't always given the choice."

"Sometimes things are taken from us," Kirsten said.

"And yet, life goes on." Allyson glanced down at the pearl ring on her finger. "And it can still be good."

Hailey felt a tap on her shoulder and turned.

"Grrrrraaaaawww!"

She screamed and jumped away from the velociraptor looming over her, and accidentally bumped Meghan's chair so that it tipped and fell backward into the laughing—*laughing*—dinosaur.

"Wait a minute." Hailey reached for the raptor's head, but Lucy beat her to it, jerking it off.

"You were supposed to try to scare the guys, not us," she scolded Micah.

"I can't see out of this thing to tell who I'm scaring."

"Sorry, ladies." Lucy smacked Micah with the raptor head. "Next to the turtles, this is his favorite part of the week. Telling him he couldn't do it would be like not giving a kid his Christmas present."

Hailey helped Meghan up.

"This has been the weirdest vacation." Meghan looked a little dazed.

"But effective?" Micah held up the dinosaur face. "I mean, don't you feel so much better now, knowing you're not about to get eaten by a real dinosaur?"

"Yes, actually." Hailey laughed. "You got me."

"Good. Then you're ready for the real thrills. Everyone back to the jeep. Your food can digest on the way down. Next we're going to see Moli'i Pond, an 800-year-old ancient Hawaiian fishpond, listed on the US National Register of Historic Places. We'll do some cleanup there for the kind folks who own this place and allow us to make this expedition. We've also got a stop scheduled at some burial grounds and a drive through Jurassic World. And if you're still with us then, we'll send you back down the mountain on a zip line."

"Hailey should go first, since she's worried about getting back in time to meet her parents." Meghan stepped aside, making room for Hailey to come to the front of the platform.

"Thanks—I think." Hailey looked over the edge, at the jungle below. "Or is this payback for pushing you into the raptor this morning?"

"I'll go first, if you don't want to," Brock volunteered. "I need to get back too. This afternoon Charlie is meeting the doctor who is going to do his prosthetics. I told him I'd be there."

"I still can't believe you arranged all that," Hailey said.

"A little luck, good timing. I was fortunate to find a doctor in Honolulu willing to meet with me and work with Charlie." Modest Brock sounded like the antithesis of his counterpart who had introduced himself to Hailey at the pool that first day.

"I bet it'll *cost* a fortune too," Meghan said.

"What good is money if you don't have something fun to spend it on? And it won't just be my money. Lucy hooked me up with a non-profit that helps pay for kids' prosthetics. So who's going first?" Brock asked, sounding suddenly uncomfortable.

"Let's do this," Ray called from farther back in the line.

"Ladies first," Meghan insisted, pulling Hailey forward.

"I'd be fine letting the guys take this one—"

Too late. The guide hooked her clip onto the line, double-checked her harness, and stepped aside. "Have fun!"

"Watch out for dinosaurs at the bottom," Meghan called as Hailey stepped off the platform."

"I knew it!" she shouted, leaning her head back and nearly flipping upside down. "I'll get you baaaack." Hailey righted herself again to better enjoy the sensation of zipping over the jungle, the wind in her face and the scenery rushing past.

The views from up here were incredible—Chinaman's Hat and the sparkling Pacific out front, lush green mountains behind her. Trees everywhere. She wished Gage had stayed to enjoy this part of the trip. He would have loved this.

Hailey stuck her feet straight out in front of her, then

swung them back and forth when she picked up a little too much speed. The sensation of flying was unlike anything she'd ever experienced. She envisioned the wind whisking away her problems as much as it was whipping her ponytail. *Be happy for both of us,* Gage had told her.

"I'm trying," Hailey shouted, her words carried away in the air rushing past. Then to herself, "I'm going home tomorrow, and I'm going to be okay. My life is going to be good."

This morning Lucy had talked a lot about affirmations, about believing in oneself, about moving forward. It was time to let go of the past and look to a new future.

As she neared the stop with the first suspension bridge Hailey wasn't at all surprised to find the velociraptor waiting for her, moving in the opposite direction from her with an odd sort of gait, stomping back and forth, swinging the bridge.

She laughed out loud. Micah was so funny. This trip had been so much more than she'd hoped for or imagined. If only she could keep all the good feels she'd collected here and take them home with her.

Hailey landed on the platform, then moved from the zip line to the bridge and started across it, heading boldly toward the raptor now halfway across. It stopped suddenly, then turned to face her. Hailey suppressed a shiver at the surprisingly realistic costume. Maybe they let Micah use one of the real ones from the set. Though she'd have thought those were all computer animations or something.

What was he up to now? She marched forward with resolve until she was only a few feet away.

"I'm not falling for that thing this time," she shouted. "Out of my way, giant lizard."

The raptor leaned forward, shaking the head of the costume free. "Would you fall for me? Again?" The headless raptor straightened, and it wasn't Micah who stood before her.

"Gage." Her traitorous heart hammered wildly. So much for letting go and moving on. *He's still here.* "You came back."

He was breathing heavily. "Don't kill me. The dinosaur was Micah's idea. I wasn't sure you'd be willing to talk to me. He thought this would get you close enough—and out here—that I'd have at least a minute or two alone with you." Gage twisted around and set the headpiece behind him on the bridge.

"I've wanted to talk to you all week," Hailey said.

"I know, and I'm sorry. For that and everything else. For not telling you the truth. For locking you out of my life instead of trusting you. I was so upset when I found out I couldn't have children that I wasn't thinking clearly. I didn't know until the day I broke our engagement. I haven't been the same since. I've been a fool and a coward and . . . so afraid to disappoint you."

Hailey pressed her lips together and nodded. It would be so easy to tell him all was forgiven, because it was. But he needed to understand the depth, and source, of her hurt. "You did disappoint me. Because you didn't trust me to love you enough. When we decided to get married, I meant that commitment for life—no matter how short or what difficulties we faced. That you thought my love was so shallow, that you thought I'd simply walk away if things weren't perfect, really hurt. It still does."

"I'm sorry," Gage said, his raptor hands held out in front of him. "I was wrong—and stupid."

She nodded again, agreeing with everything he'd said. Behind her she was vaguely aware of the others landing on the platform, probably getting ready to enter the bridge. How many people could it hold at once? *Give us a few more minutes.* "Did you read my note?"

"Yes. But not until this morning. I should have looked at

it sooner. I was afraid, about so many things. Afraid to tell you the truth, to ask so much of you. Afraid that everything I did hurt you more. And really afraid of what I'd read in your letter. Since you'd returned the ring, I could only imagine that a scathing, well-deserved reprimand accompanied it."

"No reprimand," Hailey said quietly. "You've punished yourself enough." *Just say it, Gage. Say you still love me and want to spend what time you have left together.* "You have every right to be afraid, just not of me. I can only imagine how devastating news like that must be. But even worse must be handling it on your own. I would have turned to you, Gage. I would have expected you to be by my side through it, right down to my last breath. Let me do the same for you—please."

Confusion flickered briefly in Gage's eyes.

"About that, Hailey. What you wrote in your letter, what you thought was going on with me. It isn't. I'm not sick. I'm not dying. I just can't have kids. All these years my mom thought my dad had told me before he died. She didn't know *I* didn't know. Back then the treatments for neuroblastoma were—"

"You're not sick?" *Not sick? Not terminally sick?* She squelched the hope his words had raised.

He shook his head. "Never healthier—other than my seriously bruised ego. And this." He put one dinosaur claw over his heart.

"Are you sure?" Was he still in some sort of denial? "You went to the hospital this week, Gage. Something must be wrong. You can tell me."

His face reddened. "You weren't supposed to find out about that, but since you did, I'll show you why I was there." With clumsy movements he began trying to extract himself from the dinosaur suit. "You won't believe it. Or, maybe you will, because I've been such an idiot. My injury is certainly proof of that."

"Injury?" She scanned the parts of his body that were visible.

"A dog attacked me, took a nice bite out of my leg. It happened the night you walked with Brock on the beach. I was following from the bluff above, to make sure you were okay, that you were safe."

"You were?" Hailey clasped her hands and tucked them close to her heart, feeling she might actually swoon. It was the sweetest thing Gage had told her, or done, in a long time.

"I was." Gage freed one leg. "I'd replaced Brock's note inviting you to meet him on the beach with my own. I intended to tell you that night, what I said the next day at the orphanage instead. But I was too slow. Brock was already waiting for you, and you *went with him.*"

Was that jealousy she heard in Gage's accusation? Hailey suppressed a smile. "Brock and I are only friends. Nothing more."

"I know that now," Gage said. "But I didn't know what was going on then. When you started running I thought you were trying to get away from him. I tried to follow as fast as I could and cut through some people's yards."

Gage finally succeeded in extracting his second leg from the suit. His mouth twisted in a wry grin as he showed her the large bandage covering his shin. "Most unique souvenir anyone has ever taken home from the islands."

Hailey clapped a hand over her mouth. "Oh, Gage. I'm so sorry."

He shrugged. "Me too. But at least Officer Friendly didn't take me to jail after all. My shorts had become—misplaced—during the incident, and it looked like I might get booked on charges of trespassing and indecent exposure. Fortunately

Micah vouched for me, and I was able to be released—after a couple of the most torturous shots I've ever had. I'll have to get two more rabies shots before I'm all done with this."

Hailey wrapped her arms around her middle as her mind attempted to process everything Gage had told her.

Would you fall for me again . . . I'm not sick . . .

It all seemed too good to be true. Maybe this was some sort of bizarre dream. How real could a guy in a dinosaur suit, standing on a suspension bridge over the Hawaiian jungle, be?

"You're really not sick?" she asked one more time, just to be sure, and half expecting him to evaporate instead of answer. Then she'd wake up in her bed at the resort or at home, and all of this would have been a dream.

But Gage didn't disappear. He shook his head.

"No cancer? No—anything?" *This is real. He's real.* She attempted a wobbly smile as a tear splashed on her hand.

"No cancer," Gage repeated. "But what I had as a child made it so I can't. Have. Children." He shrugged his shoulders and arms from the suit and reached for her hands. "Ever."

He isn't sick. "That's wonderful, Gage."

His brow furrowed. "Hailey?"

She tried to pull one of her hands away to wipe her nose. "I thought—since some of the others were here this week because they have these terrible illnesses—that you did too. When I heard you were at the hospital, I knew I had to be right." She sniffled, but there was no holding back the flood. "I thought you had something fatal, that you were dying."

"No." He squeezed her hands. "It just felt like it without you. Don't cry. I've made you cry so much already."

Hailey pulled away and buried her face in her hands, crying harder, though she was trying to pull herself together. She was happy. So happy, so relieved.

With guarded, awkward movements Gage maneuvered

so he was down on one knee, the one belonging to the uninjured leg. "I don't deserve you, Hailey. And I know I'm so late to ask your forgiveness, but I'm asking it anyway and asking you for even more than that—to take me as I am, though that still feels selfish of me. I can't give you children, but I'll give you everything else possible, most of all, my love. Every day of your life, for the rest of our lives. Please say you'll marry me. Please say yes." He held out his hand, her ring pinched between his thumb and forefinger. His eyes were as wet as hers.

"Yes." She nodded. "Yes, Gage." She hiccupped. Another sob came and changed to a burst of giggles. She was losing it. The lack of sleep and the stresses of the week were all coming to a head, here on a bridge above the jungle, with Gage kneeling on top of a dinosaur suit.

"Proposed to by a raptor in the middle of Jurassic Park. This will be a great story to tell our children some—" She stopped, her mouth snapping shut as she realized what she'd just said. "I didn't mean—"

But the damage was done. She could see it in Gage's fallen expression as he withdrew his hand.

No! She grabbed it before he could tuck it back inside the costume. "A great story to tell the children we *adopt* someday." She clasped his hand tightly and fell to her knees in front of him. "Or to tell our nieces and nephews. We don't have to have children, Gage. I just want *you*." She threw her other arm around him and pulled him close, their heads bent together. "Please believe me. Please."

"I do. This is just so hard, Hailey. I wanted a family too."

"I know. We can get through this together. We can still be happy. Life is still so good, Gage. I just really want to live it with you." She tilted her head and kissed him, her lips searching his, needing affirmation that he really meant his proposal, that he really wanted her still.

Seconds passed. Her heart pounded, then soared with elation when his lips moved against hers in the sweetest kiss of her life. Gage pulled her close, wrapping his arm around her. Behind them Hailey heard cheers and clapping. She didn't care. She was in Gage's arms, and she wasn't about to move.

"I love you, Hailey. Marry me. Today."

"*Today?*" She pulled back to look at him. "When? Where? You're not serious."

"I am. Kualoa Ranch does weddings too. And it appears that it's been all arranged. Our parents are all here, or yours will be here soon—I think you had something to do with that—and Meghan and Lucy took care of logistics. All you have to do is say yes, and a couple of hours from now you can be Mrs. Stevens."

Today. A day earlier than they were supposed to have been married. In Hawaii instead of New York. *Sand instead of snow. Yes!* "Yes, Gage. A thousand times yes." Hailey held out her hand, and he slipped the ring on her finger.

"Come on." He struggled to his feet, then grabbed her hand, pulled her up, and stepped the rest of the way out of the dinosaur suit. He pulled Hailey into his arms and held her tight. "I love you, Hailey Walsh. I'm sorry I've been so stupid."

"Just don't be stupid anymore," she whispered. Then louder, "I love you too, Gage."

"Let's go get married, then." He started to run-limp, towing her toward the opposite end of the bridge. "We're inseparable, starting right now. There's a tandem harness. We soar the rest of the way together."

Micah and another guide waited on the platform at the end of the bridge.

"Nice job, dinosaur man." Micah high-fived Gage, then

pulled Hailey in for a quick hug. "I love happy endings like this." He gave an exaggerated sniffle. "Seriously. If my job could be this awesome every day . . ."

The guide helped them attach the tandem harness and hook into the cables.

Gage took Hailey's hand in his and looked at her. "Ready?"

She nodded. "I have been. Just waiting for you."

"The wait is over," Gage said.

Together they stepped forward off the platform and soared over the treetops, on the way to their future together.

32

Almost Perfect

"I WASN'T ABLE to save my parents' marriage, but I helped save yours." Meghan adjusted Hailey's veil so that it hung just right over her hair. "You have no idea how satisfying this is for me."

"I might have an inkling." Hailey gave Meghan a hug, then turned to hug each of the other women in the room. "Thank you. *All* of you." She held onto her mom a little longer, appreciating her as she hadn't before this week.

"You look beautiful, Hailey. Just perfect." Mom squeezed her hands.

"Almost perfect," Meghan corrected. "There's a white spot on your nose." She stepped forward. "Let me help—"

"You can't." Hailey peered in the full-length mirror once more. "My nose is peeling. It's from the sunburn I got a few days ago." She held up her hands. "And I broke all my nails building the playground."

"None of that matters," Allyson said.

"I know." Hailey breathed in deeply and felt contentment and peace wash over her. "This isn't the wedding we planned. It's not going to be the life we planned either. But it's still almost perfect. Gage is everything I need."

"You're so lucky," Lisbeth said, a wistful smile on her face. "We all are, to have had this magical week and to end it like this."

Hailey gave Lisbeth another hug. "I wish for you every happiness." Tears burned behind Hailey's eyes. "I hope you and Brock—"

Lisbeth pulled away and shook her head. "Don't go there. Please," she added softly. "Brock and I have both agreed that it's best if we take one week at a time. Trying to look or plan too far into the future isn't a good idea right now, for either of us. But I am so *very* happy today, right now. For you."

Hailey wiped at her wet eyes and nodded, feeling a surge of love for Lisbeth.

"Time to go," Meghan said. "You don't want to keep Gage waiting. Especially because there's only one boat. Miss that, and we're in trouble."

They made their way outside, Allyson and Kirsten holding Hailey's train as they crossed the lawn and boardwalk to the waiting catamaran. Her father and Gage were already on board, standing at the back, waiting to help her and Mom up. Gage presented her with a flower lei to match the one he was already wearing, then took her hand. They sat at the head of the boat, his mother on one side, her parents on the other, and the rest of the group on the benches.

Hailey held her veil to her head during the five-minute boat ride, and the women held her train once more as they disembarked and followed the winding trail through hau trees to the white sand and sparkling water of Secret Island Beach. As they emerged from the trees she stopped, her hand squeezing Gage's as she looked up at him.

"This feels like a dream. No one gets married the day after Christmas and in a beautiful place like this."

He leaned down and kissed the top of her sunburned nose. "We do."

Gage and the others went ahead, Gage's walk still a little

stiff, while Hailey stayed back for her father to escort her up the aisle.

"Is my little girl ready for this?" he asked when the first strains of the "Hawaiian Wedding Song" reached them.

"Yes, Dad. I've been ready to marry Gage for a long time." Hailey kicked off her plain sandals—not the fancy shoes she'd planned to wear at her wedding—and started across the sand barefoot.

Micah played the ukulele, and Darren sang. Hailey blew them a kiss as she passed. Her father walked her nearly to the water, where someone had made a drawing of two turtles on the sand.

"The Honu," Micah reminded her. "Your guardian spirits, the eternal link. You both saw them, and there were two . . . I should have known then."

"I'll remember that day forever," Hailey said.

"Me too." Gage took her hand, and they stood beneath an arch of fragrant flowers and vines.

Hailey looked up at the masterpiece. "How—"

"There's another event here this evening," Meghan whispered as she came forward to straighten Hailey's veil again. "An older couple renewing their vows. Lucy and Micah are friends of the owners, so they persuaded them to let us use everything. We just have to be gone by four. So don't take too long."

"Ah . . ." Hailey suppressed a laugh. Everything made a lot more sense now. And everything was turning out so much better than she had imagined. When she'd asked her parents and Gage's mom to come, she'd believed that talking with Gage would restore their relationship and they could still have their December 27th wedding—only in Hawaii, since they would still be here. Micah had told her he could arrange for clergy to come to the resort. That would have been nice enough. *This* was spectacular.

Gage took her other hand in his, and they began their vows.

"In sickness and in health, in poverty or wealth, for better for worse." Children or no children. She was good with all of that. Come what may, they would be together. Almost perfect was enough.

33

The Love Boat

"May I cut in, please?"

Gage turned to find it was Brock who'd tapped his shoulder.

"You've been hogging the bride all night." Brock held his hand out, and Hailey took it.

"My bride, my prerogative," Gage grumbled, but stepped back all the same. "One dance. Then I get her back."

"One is about all I'm good for these days." Brock flashed a wry grin as he spirited Hailey away, farther onto the makeshift dance floor, previously known as the lanai.

The long table and the chairs had all been moved to allow for dancing. Lights were strung around the perimeter, and tiki torches lined the drive leading up to the house. Hawaiian Holidays usual—last-night luau, complete with a pig cooked in a pit—had provided plenty of food for the occasion, including enough for the *extra* guests who had wandered over throughout the evening.

Watching a few of those now—some of the homeless he'd brought food to earlier in the week—Gage realized that having the locals join in for these luaus must be a longstanding tradition. Either that, or Micah had felt the need to invite more wedding guests.

All things considered, for an impromptu wedding reception, everything had gone off without a hitch.

Gage wandered over to the drink table and served himself a glass of Hawaiian punch.

"Watching those two again, I see."

He looked up, then stepped back, putting more distance between himself and the other side of the table. "Marge." He choked on the punch as it went down.

She smiled sweetly. "Congratulations. We're sorry we didn't believe you."

"We?" Sensing more company, Gage looked right and caught sight of her sumo-wrestler husband making his way toward them. "Just so long as you didn't bring Grunt," Gage said, only half-joking.

"Grunt is at home. Guarding the place." Mack gave Gage a playful thump on the shoulder that nearly sent him sprawling.

"So you married her, but she's still dancing with the other guy?"

"I'm about to remedy that. Good to see you." *From this perspective.* Gage took a last swallow of punch, then headed toward the other side of the lanai to reclaim his bride.

Micah stopped him before he could reach her. "Hey, where are you and Hailey planning to stay tonight?"

"My mom has a hotel in Waikiki. We thought—if it's okay with you—she could stay in Hailey's bungalow, and we'd take her hotel room. We'll come back for Mom tomorrow before we all fly home. We didn't suppose you encouraged the sharing of rooms here, and I'd really prefer to sleep with my wife tonight."

"Your mom is welcome to stay," Micah said. "And, yeah, sharing of rooms is pretty much off limits. But don't drive all the way to Waikiki. I've got a better idea." He fished a set of keys out of his shorts pocket. "I've got a boat docked not too far from here. It's nothing fancy, but it's private—and it's on the water. Since you went ahead and got married in Hawaii, might as well complete the experience by spending your wedding night at sea—so to speak. Without actually leaving the dock, of course."

"Of course," Gage said. "Can't say sailing was on my wish list for tonight." He wondered what Hailey would think about staying on a boat instead of at a hotel.

"But you'll have the beach, the moonlight and stars . . . It's the *love boat*," Micah sang, or tried to. He let the suggestion hang in the air. "You don't want Hailey's only nighttime beach experience here to have been with Brock, do you?"

"No." Gage held his hand out, and Micah slapped the keys into his palm.

"Thanks." Gage curled his fingers around the keys as his eyes scanned the room for Hailey. Brock sat with Lisbeth again. "Where is my wife?" He loved the sound of that.

"Over there." Micah jerked a thumb in the opposite direction Gage had been looking. "Dancing with Charlie."

She was indeed, standing behind the boy, his wheelchair tilted back so that only the rear wheels met the floor. She was moving the chair to the beat, turning it and doing all else she could, it looked like, to make the kid sick. But he was only laughing.

"Thanks, Micah." Gage said again, looking down at the keys. "For everything. I'll never be able to repay you. Though I'm happy to pay you for use of the boat tonight."

"No need." A corner of Micah's mouth lifted. "Though there is *something* you and Hailey could do for us."

"Name it," Gage said. "We can't thank you enough."

Micah placed a hand on Gage's shoulder and turned him away from the dancing. "You weren't here Christmas morning to hear Hailey's ideas about the orphanage, but Lucy and I haven't been able to stop thinking about them."

"Interior redesign?" Gage guessed. "That's Hailey's jam. She's brilliant at it."

"It would appear so," Micah agreed. "She shared some additional ideas with us on the safari today, and we were even more excited. So what would you two think..." Micah paused, his smile broadening, "about staying another week or so and having a 'most expenses paid,' Hawaiian Holiday service honeymoon?"

34

Winter Wonderland

"Where are you taking me?" Hailey demanded, arms folded as she stared at Gage from the passenger side of the rented jeep. "My sense of direction isn't great, but even *I* know we're headed *away* from Waikiki, not toward it."

"Can't a guy surprise his wife on their wedding night?" Gage gripped the wheel with both hands and attempted a serious look as he drove.

"All right. Just so long as there isn't a dinosaur costume involved."

Gage laughed. "No reptiles—at least, I don't think so. Though I suppose there could be turtles where we're going."

"Are we staying at Turtle Bay?" Hailey had dreamed of that briefly, the morning they ate there.

"Sorry," Gage said. "Wrong husband. We're headed somewhere a little more budget friendly. You see, I bought this fixer-upper house with my wife . . ."

"Yeah. Yeah. I know." Hailey leaned her head back against the seat, thinking of their little house. Their. Little. House. *Ours. The two of us.* She loved being married already.

"Maybe we could eat at Turtle Bay tomorrow night though," Gage said, with a quick, concerned glance her direction. "I think our budget could swing that."

"Don't we have flights tomorrow?" Now she was really confused. She'd hoped to change their reservations, so they could fly together, but everything was booked so soon after the holiday. They would just have to fly home separately and meet up at the airport in New York. Disappointing, but it couldn't be helped. Now that they were married, it was back to being frugal, getting their business and/or non-profit off the ground, and making the mortgage payment.

"We do have flights," Gage said, vaguely. "Unless we cancel them."

"And rebook? I thought we agreed we couldn't afford that."

"We couldn't. Not at all." Gage's attempts to look serious were getting worse. His lips were practically smashed together, he was trying so hard not to smile. "This afternoon we couldn't afford them. But tonight . . ."

"All right, spill it." Hailey leaned forward and reached for the steering wheel, intending to turn it, but Gage beat her to it, directing the jeep off the highway.

Instead of asking where they were going, she took in their surroundings. A smallish marina of some sort, a few buildings, the beach and ocean. Not much else.

Gage parked the car and came around to her side to help her out.

Hailey accepted his hand and silently followed him down to the beach, where Gage set their overnight bags on the sand, then plopped himself down beside them. "Well, what do you think?"

Seriously? He was still messing with her, wasn't he? "If you want to chance getting your stitches infected with sand while we sleep here, then I'm good with it. Would have been nice to bring a pillow, though. Guess you'll have to do." She leaned over and punched his stomach playfully before falling on top of him.

Gage brushed the hair out of her face and kissed her. "Micah lent us his boat for the night. We're not sleeping on the beach."

"You aren't," Hailey teased. "I might want to." She returned his kiss with a fervor that said otherwise.

"About tomorrow," Gage began, some minutes later when they were both out of breath and Hailey felt like she might internally combust any second.

"And the day after that and the day after that," he continued. "What would you think of staying an extra week or two?"

Hailey sat up straight and leaned away from him. "I'd love it, but we can't afford that—unless you've had some other news, some amazing, we-just-inherited-millions-from-an-obscure-relative kind of news, that you haven't shared with me."

Gage pulled her back against his chest and wrapped his arms around her. "Micah and Lucy want you to do the remodel on the orphanage—or the dormitory, at least—right now. Whatever you've shared with them so far has them really excited. They've got more crews of laborers on their way—more Hawaiian Holiday participants for sessions in the new year—and they have money in the bank to fund the redesign. They want *you* to stay and orchestrate everything."

"Really?" Hailey jumped up. "Do you realize what this means? It's perfect. We'll have something for our portfolio and our pitch."

Gage's brow furrowed. "What pitch? What did I miss?"

"A lot." Hailey pulled him up beside her. "I'll fill you in as we walk to the boat."

"Should I be worried?" Gage picked up their bags in one hand and wrapped his other arm around Hailey.

She reciprocated, her hand behind him at his waist. They began walking along the beach toward the farthest dock.

"What would you think if we started a nonprofit?"

"Interesting," Gage said. "Go on, my business-minded wife."

Hailey grinned. He'd always been so great about that, about listening to her crazy ideas and telling her they weren't so crazy and then running with them as fast as he could. There was some back and forth, of course, but never had he rejected her plans.

"I had the idea Christmas morning," she began, then launched into a detailed list of things that would need to be done, how they should tackle those, and in what order. Renovating the orphanage so soon would be an unexpected bonus. Experience and references would be golden.

Sometime during their conversation they'd stopped walking and stood looking out at the ocean.

"I'd give you the moon if I could, Hailey." Gage raised his face to the sky as he spoke. "I can at least give you this. Let's try it. I like it. I like that we'd be using our skills and talents to make other people happy. And if it takes a while for everything to get rolling, I can keep taking drafting jobs and you can continue to do consults to keep us afloat. We'll figure out how to make it all work."

"I love you, Gage Stevens." Hailey threw both arms around him, and he swept her up in a hug, swinging her around once on the sand.

"That's all. Sorry." He set her down where she'd been. "Leg's still sore." He frowned as he glanced down at his shin.

"It was enough," Hailey said quietly. "*You* are enough."

They stood together, watching the breakers roll in and

the water lap up onto the shore, teasing them until it finally reached their feet, nipping at their toes as they stood in a swathe of moonlight.

"We should find the boat," Gage said at last.

"Yes," Hailey agreed. Her eyes lingered on the horizon, where the dark sky met the sea, barely lit by a moonbeam.

They started down the beach again, and she began to hum. It didn't look exactly like Christmas here, but it felt like it, like pure joy. And everything about the day had been like a dream, as if she was in Wonderland itself.

Gage caught the tune and began humming with her.

Holding his hand, swinging it back and forth, she felt swept away in the enchantment of the night, this place, their moments together. Sand instead of snow, warm instead of cold, but still they were walking in a winter wonderland.

35

Even Better

"CAN YOU HAND me that other paintbrush, please? The small one." Hailey leaned away from the ladder, hand extended, waiting for Gage. She was almost done touching up the new paint that had gone up in the dormitories yesterday. There were just a few more thin spots that needed her attention.

Remodeling an orphanage wasn't what many couples would consider a great honeymoon, but for her and Gage, it had been just about perfect. That they had only a few days left of the ten extra they'd booked to stay in Hawaii made her sad.

Gage grabbed the brush but held it just out of Hailey's reach. "There will be a price for that, Mrs. Stevens."

Hailey placed a hand on her hip. "And what would that be?" If only all her decorating jobs were always this fun. *They might be.* She and Gage were business partners now.

"You know my terms," Gage said in a serious tone, though his eyes were full of mischief.

"Come here, then." Hailey crooked a finger at him. Gage took a step toward her, and she reached down to grab the front of his T-shirt and pull him close. She kissed him briefly, then snatched the brush and held it out of his reach.

He frowned. "Those weren't the original terms. You seem to be cheating me."

Hailey laughed. "Full payment to come later. I promise. We just need to get this done. Lucy asked to see us this afternoon, remember. We only have about thirty minutes until we're supposed to meet her."

"Lucy, Schmucy," Gage grumbled but returned to work touching up the trim in the room.

He finished first, and when Hailey had completed her work she found him outside on the playground, holding Amura while he sat on one of the new swings.

"She needed some fresh air," Gage said. "One can only remain in a playpen for so long."

"No one's judging." Hailey kissed his forehead. "I'm going to wash up. Meet me at the car in five?"

"Sure thing, boss."

Hailey left them swinging, then went to clean the brushes. She was doing her best to keep project costs down, so that meant reusing or repurposing everything possible. If something could be washed and saved for another time, it would be.

From the kitchen window over the sink she watched Gage as he sat with Amura. He was talking to her and making her laugh. The sound carried through the open window and simultaneously melted and broke Hailey's heart.

Someday.

Lucy hadn't said much about Amura's impending adoption, only that it was in progress. Hailey wasn't certain whether she was grateful or not that Amura was still here. Both she and Gage had enjoyed spending time with her. But it was going to be hard to leave in a few days, knowing they'd never see her again.

Maybe, when she and Gage could afford it, Lucy would be able to help them find a child through one of the adoption agencies she and Micah worked with.

Hailey set a clean brush aside and reached for another, paint-filled one. Though she and Gage hadn't planned on waiting to begin their family, reality was that now they would have to. She wasn't sure what the requirements or qualifications were for adopting a child, but newlyweds in the midst of starting a new business probably weren't the best candidates.

They'd talked little about that this week. The topic of being unable to have children was still difficult for them both, particularly Gage, and Hailey didn't want to do anything that would make him feel anything less than perfect to her. They were both young. There would be time enough for children. And if they didn't get as many as they'd wanted or have them as soon as they'd planned, it would all be okay. They had each other, and they'd make whatever alternate ending they had a happy one.

Twenty minutes later they arrived at the resort. A new group of Hawaiian Holiday residents milled about the pool and inside when Gage and Hailey entered the great room. The Christmas tree had been taken down, and everything felt different, now that the others were gone.

It might have made Hailey feel a little melancholy had she not been on her honeymoon and so incredibly happy.

Yesterday she'd heard from Brock. Lisbeth's surgery had gone well. They hadn't been able to get all of her tumor, but enough of it that they felt she had a good chance at shrinking the rest through treatment. She would be in the hospital until the end of the week and was already well enough to boss Brock around.

"Hailey, Gage, thank you for coming." Lucy held her hands out to them as she crossed the room to greet them. "I know you have a lot to do at the orphanage still and little time left to do it."

"Actually," Hailey smiled, "we're ahead of schedule. My partner is pretty efficient." She squeezed Gage's hand.

"I'm glad to hear that." Lucy waved them over toward the door that led to her private office. "Let's go inside. I have another idea I hope you'll consider. Micah and I feel like your being here over Christmas was inspired for more than one reason."

Gage drew the sheet up to Hailey's shoulders, then leaned over and kissed her forehead. He smiled to himself as he watched her sleep. How could he have ever thought of letting her go? He was the luckiest man on earth.

He left her sleeping and walked out to their balcony, overlooking Turtle Bay. He'd been fortunate it was a slower time of year—and that Micah had connections—and was able to help Gage snag a room here for the last two nights in Hawaii.

Everything seemed to be falling into place perfectly, as if there was someone else orchestrating his life instead of him.

That wasn't a new concept, just one he'd thought a lot about lately. He wasn't to the point where he felt grateful for the news that had devastated him the better part of the last month, but he also wasn't in a place where it was hurting him anymore. Oddly, he was starting to feel like it wasn't such a bad thing, that it had led him to this place and people who would be dear to him the rest of his life.

After their meeting with Lucy, he and Hailey had spent a long evening walking up and down the beach, talking. What they were about to undertake would not have even been a consideration—like this trip—if he hadn't had cancer as a child, and if his illness hadn't caused the long-term consequences that it did.

Unfortunate was the word his mom had used, when referring to his condition. But was it really? Or did it just make things different from what most people experienced in the course of their lives? Was it a gift?

Gage didn't have all the answers, but he did know that his inability to have children didn't matter now like it had even a week ago. Being with Hailey made him feel like a man and a half, not half a man. She completed him in so many ways, and he felt whole and healed with her. Everything in their lives was on target to be as wonderful as they'd planned. They were simply going to be arriving at some destinations in a different manner, and a whole lot sooner than even they had planned.

The palm trees beside the balcony rustled in the night breeze. Plumeria scented the air. The moon shone overhead, a sliver compared to what it had been when they arrived. *Just like my pain. A fragment of what it was two weeks ago.* He'd been so blessed.

Gage leaned forward on the railing, looking down at the water, imagining he saw a pair of turtles swimming there. *Or were there* three *together now?* He smiled, remembering Hailey's expression of wonder that morning in the bay and imagining what it might be like to be there with her again, a year from now, with a little person between them, holding their hands and squealing with delight as the tide washed over their toes.

We'll have to return. It was a comforting thought. Like Hailey, he was going to be sad to see their time here end. Yet he was also eager to return home and begin their life there together. It was going to be different than they had planned.

It was going to be even better.

36

It's a Wonderful Life

"What an adorable little girl." The flight attendant was at least the fifth one to make a similar remark about Amura, followed by a curious look at the three of them. Red hair, brown, and black. Green eyes, blue eyes, brown. Pale skin and dark. It was obvious something didn't add up. After the long flight Hailey was tired of explaining.

Gage must have been too. "Thanks," he said. "We think she's pretty special." He took Amura from Hailey so she could start packing things up before they landed.

"That's your fault, you know," he whispered as the attendant passed. "You could have dressed her in pajamas instead of this fancy dress. People can't help but notice her."

"She can't meet her new family in pajamas. First impressions are important—even for a baby." Hailey stuffed the empty bottle into the pocket of the diaper bag. "Besides, you bought her that outfit, and I wanted to see her wear it—at least once." Hailey felt a tug of sorrow.

Amura seemed to be having a growth spurt, evident in the ten days since their wedding. Hailey had noticed it even more the last few days, since Lucy had called Hailey and Gage into her office to tell them she'd decided it was in Amura's best interest to return to the mainland, instead of being adopted by a local family. Lucy felt she had found the perfect couple to adopt Amura and wanted their opinion.

It had been a whirlwind and monumental last few days. And it wasn't over yet.

"You okay?" Gage put his arm around Hailey.

"I will be," she said. "This trip has been magical." Joyous, meaningful, unforgettable. Hawaiian Holidays had lived up to its promise and more. "I guess I'm just sad that it's coming to an end. And I'm nervous for Amura. What if they don't love her?"

"They will. The real question is—what if your family hasn't forgiven me? Particularly your brute of a brother. Never met someone so overprotective in my life."

"As brothers should be." She patted Gage's arm. "Don't worry. They all still love you."

"Let's hope so." He winced as he removed Amura's hand from the top of his shirt, and the chest hair she'd grasped. "She is a special little girl. With a really strong grip." He shook his head as he looked into her large, brown eyes. "That's okay. I didn't need those hairs anyway."

The plane descended into Syracuse. Hailey looked out the window, seeing brown and white instead of the blue and green she'd grown used to the last couple of weeks.

"Ready to be cold?" Gage asked as they gathered their belongings.

"No." Hailey shook her head. "Not at all. Though I can't wait to be home with you—*our* home finally."

"Me too." He kissed her swiftly but with a look that promised more later.

She felt a shiver that had nothing to do with cold.

"Let's wait to get off until everyone else has," Gage suggested.

"Good idea." Hailey told herself they were waiting

because it was easier than navigating the crowd with a baby, but she knew differently as she adjusted Amura's knit booties and wiped drool off her. They were both nervous.

When there was no one left but them, no more excuses to be had, Gage stood and made his way to the aisle. Hailey followed, wanting to hold Amura, but knowing Gage did as well and that maybe he needed her more right now, as he faced her family again. When he buckled Amura into the carrier strapped to his chest, Hailey didn't protest.

They made their way up the Jetway, hands clasped, in this together. They walked more slowly than usual as they made their way past the other terminals, past security, toward the baggage claim.

They turned a corner, and Hailey felt her heart in her throat as she saw the sign and heard the cheering.

Welcome Home, Stevens Family!

Her sisters swarmed her then, followed by their offspring, little fingers wrapping around her knees, threatening to knock her over.

"Aunt Hailey, you're home!"

"Aunt Hailey, you got married without me," from her nieces who'd looked forward to being flower girls.

"Aunt Hailey, your new baby is so pretty."

Beside her, Gage was getting his own ribbing.

"Didn't waste any time, I see," her brother teased. "Talk about a honeymoon baby."

There were more hugs and questions and congratulations. Everyone wanted to see Amura, who started to cry because of all the excitement.

A representative from the adoption agency was there as well, to greet them and to see that Amura had arrived safely, that she had a proper car seat, and that all else was off to a good start. There would be more paperwork and visits later, but through the grace of God and Lucy and Micah's generosity with expenses, Amura was on her way to being a Stevens. *Well and truly on her way to being ours.*

Once again, Hailey almost felt the need to pinch herself. First Gage was hers, and now Amura. She was so blessed.

It was over an hour before the three of them were settled in the quiet of Hailey's car. Another two before they arrived in Chaumont and were home, where another sign welcoming them and specifically welcoming Amura hung from the front porch.

In their absence her mom had been by and set up a hand-me-down crib from one of Hailey's sisters. It wasn't the nursery Hailey had envisioned, and Amura looked nothing like the child Hailey had imagined when they finally tucked her in that night. She was even more beautiful, and Hailey already loved her more than she would have believed possible.

"And now, Mrs. Stevens, I believe it's our turn to go to bed. In *our* bedroom." Gage swept Hailey off her feet and carried her into the other room. The curtains on the bay window were still open, and snow was falling, lit by the historic lamps lining Main Street.

Gage set her down before the window. It looked like Christmas all over again and reminded her of one of her favorite holiday movies.

"There's one thing we have to do before we go to bed." Hailey dug through her bag from the flight, searching until she found the gratitude notebook. "I could write all night."

"Me too." Gage wrapped his arms around her from behind. "But I have other plans. Just write one thing. Tomorrow you can make a whole list of things you're grateful for."

"Just one? After a day like today, how can I possibly choose?" Hailey picked up the pen and opened the notebook.

"I'll help." Gage held his hand out for the notebook.

Hailey surrendered it to him, along with the pen. He wrote quickly, then handed it back to her.

We are thankful for alternate endings and that it really is a wonderful life.

A final note,

Thank you for reading *Hawaiian Holiday*.

I continue to appreciate those who take the time to read my stories and those who post reviews as well. You make it possible for me to continue doing what I love.

If you would like more information about my other books and future releases, please visit:

www.michelepaigeholmes.com. You can also follow me on Twitter at @MichelePHolmes.

Happy reading!

Michele

Michele Paige Holmes spent her childhood and youth in Arizona and northern California, often curled up with a good book instead of out enjoying the sunshine. She graduated from Brigham Young University with a degree in elementary education and found it an excellent major with which to indulge her love of children's literature.

Her first novel, *Counting Stars*, won the 2007 Whitney Award for Best Romance. Its companion novel, a romantic suspense titled *All the Stars in Heaven*, was a Whitney Award finalist, as was her first historical romance, *Captive Heart*. *My Lucky Stars* completed the Stars series.

In 2014 Michele launched the Hearthfire Historical Romance line, with the debut title, *Saving Grace*. *Loving Helen* is the companion novel, with a third, *Marrying Christopher*, followed by the companion novella *Twelve Days in December*. The Hearthfire Scottish Historical Romances include *Yesterday's Promise*, *A Promise for Tomorrow*, and *The Promise of Home*.

When not reading or writing romance, Michele is busy

with her full-time job as a wife and mother. She and her husband live in Utah with their five high-maintenance children, and a Shitzu that resembles a teddy bear, in a house with a wonderful view of the mountains.

You can find Michele on the web:
MichelePaigeHolmes.com
Facebook: Michele Holmes
Twitter: @MichelePHolmes

www.ingramcontent.com/pod-product-compliance
Lightning Source LLC
LaVergne TN
LVHW021803060526
838201LV00058B/3221